THE BESTSELLING *CASTLE* SERIES!

Don't miss the hilarious adventures of
the Realms Perilous, in all their madcap glory . . .

Read the entire *Castle* series by
John DeChancie!

Our adventures begin at

CASTLE PERILOUS

. . . where magic and mayhem lurk behind
every door—all 144,000 of them.

CASTLE FOR RENT

While the king's stuck in a time warp,
Castle Perilous is overtaken—by nasty blue demons!

CASTLE KIDNAPPED

Can Lord Incarnadine protect the Castle
from magic gone awry?

CASTLE WAR!

War is hell—especially when the enemy
is a hostile army of alter egos!

CASTLE MURDERS

How do you catch a killer in a castle
with 144,000 back doors?

D0190988

Ace Books by John DeChancie

CASTLE PERILOUS
CASTLE FOR RENT
CASTLE KIDNAPPED
CASTLE WAR!
CASTLE MURDERS
CASTLE DREAMS
CASTLE SPELLBOUND
THE KRUTON INTERFACE

The Skyway Trilogy

STARRIGGER
RED LIMIT FREEWAY
PARADOX ALLEY

CASTLE
DREAMS

John DeChancie

ACE BOOKS, NEW YORK

If you purchased this book without a cover, you should be aware that this book is stolen property. It was reported as "unsold and destroyed" to the publisher, and neither the author nor the publisher has received any payment for this "stripped book."

This book is an Ace original edition,
and has never been previously published.

CASTLE DREAMS

An Ace Book / published by arrangement with
the author

PRINTING HISTORY
Ace edition / April 1992

All rights reserved.
Copyright © 1992 by John DeChancie.
Cover art by Robert Grace.
This book may not be reproduced in whole or in part,
by mimeograph or any other means, without permission.
For information address: The Berkley Publishing Group,
200 Madison Avenue, New York, NY 10016.

ISBN: 0-441-09414-7

Ace Books are published by The Berkley Publishing Group,
200 Madison Avenue, New York, New York 10016.
The name "ACE" and the "A" logo
are trademarks belonging to Charter Communications, Inc.

PRINTED IN THE UNITED STATES OF AMERICA

10 9 8 7 6 5 4 3 2

To my mother, Mrs. Gene DeChancie

Oh, tell me not in mournful numbers,
  "Life is but an empty dream;
For the soul is dead that slumbers,
  And things are not what they seem!"

Life is real! Life is earnest!
  And the grave is not its goal:
"Dust thou art, to dust returnest,"
  Was not spoken of the soul.

                    —Longfellow

FOREWORD

YET ANOTHER CASTLE BOOK!

Again the mystery, again the enigma of Castle Perilous, presented once more in a highly colorful tale of adventure, written by "John DeChancie," the purported author of all the Castle romances, who, unless this investigator has completely botched the job of ferreting him out, does not exist in any known world, i.e. in any of the worlds accessible via the castle.

Readers of previous books in this series will by now need no introduction to the castle, its residents, or its mysteries. However, as series books are sometimes read out of sequence, perhaps a capsule summary of the complex setting in which these stories are laid will serve as a pocket travel guide, as it were, to the world—and the myriad universes—of Castle Perilous.

Castle Perilous is a fortress atop a citadel bestriding the Plains of Baranthe, situate in a region known as the Western Pale, in a world bleak and drear. Nothing definite may be said of the castle's size—save that it is vast; nor of its structure—save that it beggars description. It is no ordinary castle. Its external aspects shift and slide and rearrange, as do its labyrinthine interior spaces. It is the ultimate maze, one sometimes as terrifyingly dangerous as it is confounding. But this indeterminate aspect of its nature is not the only peculiarity; for beyond almost every door and window, through almost every portal within the castle's tumultuous enclosures, lies another world. And through these portals come creatures of every description—fanged and furred they come; scaled and scrofulous they slither forth; beings fantastic and *outré*, some more horrific than the phantoms haunting the sweatiest nightmare.

Not all are monsters; in point of fact most visitors are human; and, indeed, most of the nonhuman "Guests" are decent enough sorts, in sharp contradistinction to their terrifying appearance.

For all its bizarre nature, however, Castle Perilous is a proper castle, and even boasts a king. His name is Incarnadine, Lord of the Western Pale, and, by the grace of the gods, King of the Realms Perilous. If understatement can sometimes be more eloquent than hyperbole, and more convincing, let us say that he is something of a magician, drawing on the castle itself as the source of his thaumaturgical powers. A gracious host as well, he cherishes his Guests and makes them eternally welcome.

What is the castle, exactly, and why does it exist? That is a long story. The tales of Castle Perilous are as endless as the worlds it contains. Only a relative few of them have been set down. . . .

. . . Which brings us up to this present volume.

This is the sixth installment of a work which bears the overarching title *The Eidolons of the King*, and, although past volumes have presented some problems regarding textual exegesis, this is the first book that, bids fair—if its numerous puzzles continue to resist critical explication—to become that bane of scholars down through the ages: the apocryphal work.

For all of the castle adventures thus far have been based to some extent on truth. The tales told in preceding books were in fact true stories, so far as this castle scribe has been able to ascertain. Indeed, some of the castle's more harrowing events are forever etched in acid on the copperplate of my memory. But this is not the case with the "events" related in this particular castle book. No such happenings have been recorded in Perilous's annals. No such drama ever unfolded within its dark purlieus.

What, then, to make of this book? Is it simply a spurious work, written by some plagiarist with an eye toward a quick advance on royalties and sold to the hapless publisher, who might know the real author—say he is a reclusive crank— only by correspondence? I think this unlikely. Yet I have no explanation for this volume's being different in style and content from the previous ones. Conundrums abound. What are we to make of its (if you will forgive the term) "postmodernist" touches: for instance, the chapters labeled "Spot Quiz No.——" and numbered accordingly? How to explain the spurious "footnotes," most of which make no sense? Are these mere japes? Why is the vernacular used so extensively in the eschatological sections? Indeed, why is it that some of the questions in the "quizzes" have nothing to do with the text? These purported study exercises seem to be mockeries. We must conclude as much, for it is hard to credit the notion that this highly romantic bit of light entertainment was actually intended as a serious text for the study of literature. Diverting it may be; Art it certainly is not, despite its ham-handed pretensions.

Questions, questions. I, for one, harbor no hope that they will eventually be answered. For like the castle itself, the

Castle series is an enigma. Of doubtful provenance, it provokes as much as it entertains. Analyze, explicate, and interpret as is your wont, but do all at your peril, for these books seem to justify the claims of the "deconstructionist" critics, who hold that, at bottom, any given text is not susceptible of reduction to any unambiguous meaning. In short: all texts are at once meaningful and meaningless, and there is no final sorting out of their uncertainties, for all the critical acumen we bring to bear on them. Like it or not, we must face the fact that there is an intrinsic uncertainty principle even in the humanistic field of belles-lettres.

All of the above notwithstanding, this is an entertaining book, like its predecessors. Setting aside its stylistic crudities, it reads well; the pace is quick, and we are compelled to turn its pages to see what happens next. We could do worse for our light reading fare. . . .

I shall say no more about it. Here, then, is *Castle Dreams*, puzzling as it is, apocryphal though it may be. In the end, the question of its authenticity could be moot. For Castle Perilous contains not simply a multitude of worlds, but a multitude of *possible* worlds.

Who is to say that the events herein related did not happen in one of them? Certainly not I.

                    Osmirik—Royal Scribe and Librarian

CASTLE—GAMING HALL

"GOING TO THE TOAD-FLING tomorrow?"

"I beg your pardon?"

Linda Barclay, pretty, blond, and blue-eyed—sorceress par excellence and general-utility magician—looked up from her bridge hand and regarded her partner, Gene Ferraro, with an expression of bemused hauteur. This reaction was something of a pose, a defensive posture, now almost automatic, against what she suspected was imminent: more standard Ferraro wisecracking.

She said, "Am I going to the *what*?"

"Toad-fling," Gene said, carefully aligning his cards as he studied them. "Good Will Turkey Shoot. World Cup Spitball Meet. Whatever they're calling it."

"You mean the All-Worlds Jousting Tournament?" asked Deena Williams, seated to Linda's left. Turning her dark head slightly, she directed her next remark to the strange creature sitting directly across from her: a large, white-furred beast, who happened to be her partner in this rubber. "Your call, Snowclaw."

"Snowclaw" was an understandable moniker in light of

the creature's long, icy-white claws. Unwieldy as they appeared, they in no way inhibited the casually deft sorting by suit of a hand of bridge.

Snowclaw gave a sarcastic grunt. "Who dealt this mess?"

"You always complain," Gene said. "Every hand. Which leads me to believe, you clever beast, that it's some kind of psychological stratagem."

"Some kind of what?" Snowclaw heaved a sigh. "Pass."

"Don't think you're putting anything over on anyone."

"Toad-fling," Linda said disapprovingly. "How cruel to toss helpless toads."

"Nonsense," Gene said. "Your regulation flinging toad is bred for the job. They don't mind a bit. In fact, they live to be flung. It fulfills their purpose in life."

"The SPCA should hear about this," Linda said. "I have half a mind to report it myself. Three spades."

"What's this toad-flingin' stuff, anyway?" Deena was curious to learn. "I thought it was knights on horses runnin' at each other with spears. Pass."

"Lances," Gene corrected. "Well, I heard they've de-emphasized the traditional combat angle. Now it's mostly track-and-field. Sort of a medieval Olympics—though they do still hold the joust. And a contestant still stands a chance of getting his neck broken. Four no-trump."

"Or hers," Linda said. "They have a woman's joust, too. Four no-trump, Gene? You sure are adventurous today. Remember, we're vulnerable."

"Too late," Deena said. "No takin' back bids."

"Going for the slam?" Snowclaw speculated. "Need a little danger, eh?"

Gene let out a breath. "It's been so damned boring around here lately. I crave excitement once in a while."

Snowclaw said, "I've been getting a little antsy myself, now that you mention it. Pass."

"Speaking of adventurism. Maybe you're *not* playing possum."

"What's a possum?"

Snowclaw looked capable of handling any excitement that might come his way. A cross between a polar bear and a bipedal cat, he had fierce yellow eyes over a snoutful of wicked teeth. For all that, his disposition seemed amiable enough.

There were other castle Guests in the Gaming Hall. At one chess table, Cleve Dalton and Lord Peter Thaxton had locked horns in an especially desperate endgame. They sat unmoving, eyes on the board. In another corner, Melanie McDaniel—russet-haired and freckle-faced—strummed a guitar, singing some Scots ballad or another. She played well, but her alto voice squeaked in the upper registers. Nevertheless, five listeners sat around her in cross-legged appreciation.

" 'All this, our South, stinks of peace,' " Gene said.

Deena frowned suspiciously. "Are you quotin' poetry again?" She cocked her head toward Linda. "He's quotin' poetry again."

"Right, but I wrote it," Gene said.

"Liar," Linda said casually.

"Oh, all right. It was actually penned by one of the immortal bards. A laureate among poets."

When no one obliged, Deena reluctantly asked, "Oh, yeah? Who?"

"Geraldo."

"Get out."

"No, really. It was during his Futurist period. Your call, Linda."

"Five diamonds."

"One ace is all you have?" Snowclaw was amused.

" 'Cept for the one up my sleeve, you stinker."

Snowclaw chuckled. "We'll just let you guys hang yourselves."

"Goin' for the slam," Deena said. "You're right, Snowy. We gonna watch 'em twist slowly in the wind. I pass."

"Gene, why don't you go off somewhere," Linda said, "and get yourself into something? Take Snowy, go exploring. Pick a world, any world. After all, the castle has a hundred forty-four thousand of them."

Gene leaned back and scratched his left thigh, tugging at the stretchable material of his green tights. "Hell, we've done that. Just last week we hiked off into that aspect with the ruined temples in a sort of jungle setting. Know the one I mean?"

"I know of several," Linda said.

"The ones that look vaguely like Angkor. Through the portal near the stairwell to the King's Tower."

"Oh, that one. Anything interesting?"

Gene shrugged. "Ruins. Jungle. Great for archaeologists. Otherwise, it was pretty boring, and the mosquitoes were as big as hang-gliders."

"I'm still itching," Snowy said.

"After we came out of there," Gene went on, "we tried a few more aspects. But they were washouts, too. Maybe we've explored all the interesting ones."

"I find that hard to believe," Linda said.

"Maybe I just need a change."

"Why don't you go back home for a little vacation? How are your parents, by the way?"

"They're in Florida for the winter."

"Go there."

"Don't care for Florida in the winter. Or the summer."

"Go to California. You haven't been there since—" Linda realized too late she was treading sensitive ground.

"Since Vaya threw me over to be a biker moll," Gene said.

"Sorry. Didn't mean to bring up painful memories."

"Oh, it's all right. After all, she was a barbarian queen when I found her,* and after all attempts at civilizing, she reverted to type. I just hope she's happy."

"Do you think she's still in southern California?"

"The club she joined is based in L.A., but she could be anywhere," Gene said as he made a minute adjustment in the arrangement of his cards. "And who knows if she stayed with that particular fraternity of motorcycle aficionados."

Deena asked, "When did you last hear from her?"

"I haven't heard from her since that letter telling me she was dropping out of UCLA."

"Maybe you should go look for her," Linda said.

Gene scowled. "Whatever for? As I said, I hope she's found happiness. As a tribal queen, she was used to being serviced by a cohort of husbands and male concubines. Mayhap a biker gang is just her cup of tea."

"You sound just a little bitter," Linda said.

"Do I? I'm not. Not at all."

The binding continued, Gene calling with five no-trump, Linda telegraphing her two kings by Blackwood convention: "Six hearts."

"Pass," Deena said. "Your bid, Gene, honey. And just remember, there's always another fish in the ocean."

"I hate fish. Oh, what the bloody hell—seven no-trump."

Linda rolled her eyes to the high-vaulted ceiling. "Gene, you shouldn't have."

Snowclaw chortled. "A grand slam! You're never going to make it, good buddy."

"Live dangerously, I say. What else have I got to occupy

Castle Kidnapped (New York, Ace Books, 1989).

my time? Besides, it's a verbal contract, and, as everyone knows—"

"Gene," Linda said, "there's no excuse for boredom. You live in Castle Perilous, which just happens to be the most interesting place in the entire universe—in the whole darn omniverse, or whatever you call the big thing that contains all the littler universes."

"Multiverse." Gene gave a tiny shrug. "Well, as the Bauhaus boys said, less is more . . . more or less."

Snowclaw blinked. "Eh?"

"I never liked their movies," Linda said.

"You should take up golf, Gene," a new voice broke in.

The bridge players turned to regard lean, wiry Cleve Dalton, who was sitting back after making a move that had been prefaced by a good fifteen minutes of thought. Dalton had the face of a Yankee storekeeper and the manner of a high-end-billable-hour lawyer, though in his pre-Perilous life he'd been a literary agent.

Gene said, "But you guys gave it up."

Dalton pointed to his opponent. "He did, not me."

Deena asked, "You really swear off for good, Lord Peter?"

Lord Peter Thaxton looked up from the chess board. Dressed in a maroon smoking jacket with ascot, he was light-haired and distinguished-looking. Although he likely hadn't seen forty yet, his face was the sort that might have looked middle-aged at twenty-five.

"I'll never swing a mashie niblick again."

"Or a brassie, or a cleek," Dalton added.

"None of those items."

"Lord Peter, you always hated playing," Gene said, "yet you always let Mr. Dalton goad you into it."

"No more," Lord Peter said. "I shall not be playing golf again. Ever."

"He means it," Dalton said gravely, nodding. "Ever since he solved the Peele Castle murders, he's been impossible."*

"Mr. Dalton," Linda said, "you can surely find another golf partner."

"Oh, I play a few holes with Rashid occasionally. But it's just not the same. Half the fun was listening to his lordship swear."

"I'm glad to have provided you with so many hours of amusement," Lord Peter said dryly.

"You did, old boy. You did."

"Though hereafter you'll have to look elsewhere for fun and games, I'm afraid."

"But I can still hear you cuss when I beat you at chess."

"This one's not over. Don't take a henhouse census just yet, old man."

"Merely a matter of time, milord."

Lord Peter merely grunted as he studied the board.

"Well," Gene said, "something will come along. Something always does. And then I regret that things aren't boring any more. Meanwhile, I try to avoid boring myself and others."

"You're about as boring as a ten-car pileup," Deena said. "Is that it, Mr. Bridge Wiz, or are we gonna have to go around with this nonsense again?"

"Yes, ma'am. Who leads?"

"I'm dummy," Linda said.

"Then I lead," Snowclaw said. He laid down the six of hearts.

"By the way," Gene said, "where's Incarnadine been lately?"

"Who knows?" Linda said. "As usual, he's had business off in one of his many universes."

---

*Castle Murders (New York, Ace Books, 1991).

"A finger in every cosmological pie."

"For a king, he does get around."

Melanie finished her Scots ballad, smiled at the applause, then launched into a Breton folk song.

The hand went badly for Gene and Linda. With Linda's hand as dummy, Gene played a club to her queen and ran the jack of diamonds. He played cagily enough after that, testing clubs, running them, then testing hearts by playing his eight to the dummy's queen.

He took every trick but the last. The defenders were one card too strong in hearts, Deena spoiling with her jack. The contract was blown.

"Rats," Gene said mildly, throwing in his hand.

"You should've been content with the little slam," Snowclaw said.

"Content," Gene mused.

"You seem kinda troubled, chum."

"*Weltschmerz.*"

"What's that?"

Linda said, "Sounds German. Gene, you're always using foreign words to show off."

"Yeah, that's me, your basic intellectual snob. You ought to hear me swear in Sanskrit."

"Is that a town?" Snowclaw asked.

"You're thinking of Scranton," Gene said. "And I've uttered mighty oaths there, too." Gene slowly got to his feet. "Well, I think I'll take a walk."

"Want some company?" Snowclaw asked.

"No, thanks, big guy. I think I want to solo this time. Got to do some thinking."

"Suit yourself."

"See you later, people," Gene said in general farewell, waving as he strolled away.

Snowclaw watched him leave, then shook his massive

head. "I dunno. I'm kind of worried about him. He's been acting funny lately."

"Cabin fever," Linda said. "You hang around the castle too much, you get it."

Melanie walked over. A steel string was dangling from her guitar.

"Busted my high-E," she said. "I'll have to go back home to find another."

"No need for that," Linda said. She sat back, crossed her arms, and closed her eyes. Something materialized on the card table—a small packet.

Melanie reached for it eagerly. "Bless my soul, a new guitar string!" In fact, she was not in the least surprised, having witnessed Linda's materialization talents many times. "Thanks, Linda."

"No problem," Linda said, then yawned. Recovered, she asked, "Where are your kids?"

As if on cue, two bonneted nursemaids, each bearing a swaddled infant, entered the hall.

"Here they are!" Melanie said, running to meet them. She took one of the babies and carried it back to the table.

"Can you tell them apart yet?" Linda asked.

"Always could," Melanie said, holding the infant up. "This one's Rafe. Want to hold him?"

"Me? Sure!"

"Hey, I want one of those," Deena said.

"Your own, or one of these?"

"Both, but for now, I'll take this one's brother."

"You get Gareth. Here, Linda. Be sure to support his head. Like this, see?"

Linda gingerly accepted the precious burden. "Oh, he's a heavy little rascal, isn't he?"

Melanie took the other baby and went to Deena. "They're both gaining weight fast."

Deena expertly enfolded Gareth in her arms.

Linda tickled Rafe's tiny dimpled chin. "Hey, there, kiddo." Not yet cognizant of humorous gestures, Rafe was dismayed.

"Thank you!" Melanie called after the nursemaids as they left the room. To Linda she said, "They eat like lumberjacks. My boobs are always sore."

"You're lucky to have enough milk to breast-feed," Deena said.

"Breast-feeding is best for babies if it's possible. But it's hard to nurse twins. By the way, where was Gene off to?"

"Nowhere in particular," Linda told her.

"He's been looking kind of depressed lately."

"It really hasn't shown until recently, but he's been unhappy since Vaya ditched him," Linda said. "He won't admit it, but she was the love of his life."

"She must have been something."

"A real bombshell."

With eyebrows arched appreciatively, Dalton said, "I'll second that."

"Ever since," Linda went on, "Gene's been traipsing through one castle aspect after another, trying to find something to take his mind off her. As I said, he'd never admit it, but it's the truth."

"When did he lose her?" Melanie wanted to know.

"Shortly before you came to the castle, I think it was."

"I don't understand you humans," Snowclaw said.

Linda turned her head. "What don't you understand, Snowy?"

"Mating. I mean, the way humans carry on about it."

"How is it handled in your world? I don't think I've ever asked before."

"Handled?"

"How is it . . . uh, you know . . . done?"

Snowclaw shrugged. "Well, you just do it. It's something that's got to be done, and you just go out and get it over with, that's all. And then you go back home and sleep for a week."

"I see. Um . . ."

"Maybe that's preferable," Dalton commented. "No fuss, no hearts and flowers."

"Maybe it's the best way," Linda said, "but it doesn't sound like very much fun."

"Fun?" Snowclaw said dubiously. "What does fun have to do with it?"

Linda began, "Well, you—" Then she thought better of it. "Uh, Snowy, maybe you'd better talk to Gene about this."

"Anything you say, Linda. Actually, I'm not all that interested in the subject, if you want to know the truth."

Dalton interjected, "Sometimes I think the subject isn't worthy of all the attention that's usually paid it."

"Anyway," Linda said, "I wish Gene would forget about the past. He's been so glum lately he hasn't been much fun at all. One thing he knows how to do is liven things up. When he's in the right mood."

"He'll get over her," Melanie said. "Just like I got over the father of these little joy-bundles."

"You don't still think of Chad?" Linda asked pointedly.

Melanie gave a wan smile. "Oh, every once in a while. Sometimes, at night, when the castle is quiet . . ." Melanie suddenly frowned. "You know, Linda, for months now I've been telling you all the secrets of my love life, and just now it suddenly struck me that I know zero about yours. Fair is fair."

Linda snorted. "Me? What love life?"

"Oh, come on."

"I've been ditched so many times I've thought of buying a backhoe."

"I think you did mention a boyfriend once."

"Yeah, I had one or two of those, and even a fiancé. But it all came to zilch zip."

"I feel as though I'm eavesdropping," Dalton said, eyes on the chessboard.

"I got no dirt to hide, no scandal," Linda said. "Kind of wish I did."

Melanie struck a pose. "Meanwhile I must struggle with the stigma of the Unwed Mother," she said, giving the line a dramatic reading.

"Aw, nobody cares about that any more," Linda said.

"I do. I still believe in marriage. Call me old-fashioned."

"Like sex," Dalton said, "and love, for that matter, marriage is beyond the realm of fashion. It's a necessary institution. Always was, always will be."

"You're an old fogey, Mr. Dalton," Linda said.

"My dear, you are quite right. And I glow with pride of it."

Snowclaw asked, "Just what is marriage, anyway?"

There was an awkward silence.

Dalton began, "Well, it's . . ."

There was a commotion in the corridor. Shouts, then murmuring voices.

"I wonder what's up?" Linda said.

"I'll go see," Melanie said and hurried to the open door.

"Maybe it's the excitement Gene was looking for," Dalton speculated. "In Castle Perilous, you don't have to wait very long for some."

"I don't like excitement," Deena said nervously. "I like it when it's quiet."

Linda said, "I kind of get nostalgic for the calmer periods

myself, sometimes, especially when the sludge starts hitting the whirling blades."

"Yeah, I can do without that sludge stuff," Deena said, scowling. "Ever since I come here it's been flyin'. First it was the Blue Meanies invadin', then it was demons, then crazy people comin' out of mirrors scarin' everybody."* Deena shook her head. "I don't need that."

"It does get interesting around here at times," Dalton admitted. "But it's good for the circulation. Gets the blood racing. It's always good to—"

"Hah *hah!*"

Dalton regarded his chess opponent, from whom the outburst had come. "What on earth has got into you?"

Lord Peter sat back, a triumphant smirk on his lips. "I moved!"

"Well, congratulations. What did you move?"

"Bishop to queen's three. There. You're in check."

Dalton studied the board. "So I am."

"You always manage to squirm out of it, but this time I've got you. You're hemmed in on all sides. You must either move your king or take the bishop with the queen, but doing the latter will put your queen in jeopardy. And if you move your king, it's only a matter of time before I corner you." Lord Peter folded his arms and gloated.

"What a jam," Dalton said appreciatively. "Quite a nice little trap you set for me."

"And have just sprung mercilessly."

"So you have, so you have. Unless . . ."

Lord Peter sat up. "Unless?"

"Well, if I'm not mistaken, if I take your king's bishop with my queen's, you're in check . . . and—unless I'm

---

Castle for Rent and *Castle War!* (New York, Ace Books, 1989 and 1990, respectively).

entirely misapprehending the strategic situation—that's mate."

Lord Peter saw with horror that Dalton was right. "Impossible!"

"I would not kid his lordship."

Lord Peter looked ill. "I think I'll go to my room and blow my bloody brains out."

"Here, here, that's hardly called for. Besides, you'll have the chambermaids all upset."

Lord Peter thought it over. "You're right, they'll refuse to step into the place and there'll be no end of mess." He gave the matter more consideration. "I'll throw myself off the King's Tower."

"Now you're being reasonable."

The giggling from Deena and Linda quickly faded as Melanie came running into the room. They saw the look on her face.

"Melanie, what's wrong?" Linda asked uneasily.

"It's the servants," Melanie said grimly. "They're saying something happened to Lord Incarnadine. Word came through from the aspect he's in."

"My God, what—?"

"They're saying . . ." Melanie swallowed hard and tried again. "They're saying he's dead."

KEEP—NEAR THE QUEEN'S TOWER—
LOWER LEVELS

LUGGING A HUGE SHEAF of fan-folded paper—a computer printout—Gene trudged the hallways of Castle Perilous, looking for a doorway into an interesting universe. His explorations of the past two weeks hadn't turned up a portal worth spitting into, and this outing was no exception.

He stopped. Before him stood an anomaly: an archway that opened onto a pleasant landscape of trees, grass, shrubs, and bright sunlight. The anomaly consisted in the fact that this innocuous scenery did not lie outside the castle in the normal sense. It was part of another world, one belonging to a universe entirely separate from the one that the castle occupied. In the castle nomenclature, this doorway to a strange cosmos was an "aspect."

He consulted the printout. It was a list of aspects with names and descriptions, grouped according to location in the castle. Gene thumbed through the pages covering the 14th floor of the keep. There were hundreds of listings, and the locations were somewhat vague. For instance: "Twelve paces east, along common bearing-wall between Tinker's

Stall and Queen's Ladies' Sewing Room: to right of foliated pilaster."

Big help. There were hundreds of empty rooms on this floor. No one knew which had been what a millennium or two ago, when this catalogue of aspects been compiled (the data had come out of an ancient book in the castle library and had recently been sorted by the castle's mainframe computer).

But Gene thought he had this aspect pegged.

"'Arcadia,'" he read aloud from the printout. "'Clement, peaceful; salubrious climate. Fauna: small and inoffensive. Population: by all indications uninhabited. Flora: extensive, variegated. Otherwise undistinguished.'"

Another parklike aspect, of which the castle had thousands. Pleasant, good for picnics and outings. Hills, trees, and grass. Of little interest to a man hungering for high adventure.

Gene moved on.

He had changed from castle clothes—the usual neo-medieval attire—to an all-weather one-piece outdoor suit that Linda had conjured for him, at his behest and to his specifications. Fashioned of a sturdy synthetic material and dyed in camouflage, it featured numerous zippered pockets and a wide utility belt. The belt had pouches holding compass and other accouterments, along with a hunting knife and scabbard. With hiking boots and backpack, he was set for any climate and terrain, within certain limits, from high desert to subarctic tundra. Very hot and very cold climates would be problematical—but of course the choice of world was his.

He simply couldn't decide.

The backpack bulged with a week's rations, and his canteen held a three-day supply of water. The trouble was that he didn't know quite what he had in mind. Was this a recreational outing? Just a backpacking trip? If so, perhaps he merely wanted to spend a week alone and watch fish break the crystalline surface of a mountain lake; or observe a canopy of silent, alien stars slowly wheeling; or look for fossils in the uplifted limestone beds of ancient seas; or maybe just contemplate the involuted folds of his navel. . . .

Then again, maybe he actually wanted to explore an inhabited aspect, one with an interesting culture that merited scrutiny. It might be entertaining to find an aspect set in a historical period similar to one of Earth's. A rough-and-tumble milieu. A war.

Was that what he hungered for? Violence? Sobering thought. He didn't think of himself as particularly bloodthirsty. True, he liked proving himself with a sword, and had parried and lunged in many a fencing duel—but all of his fighting had been in one cause or another: defending his friends and the castle against invaders, or overthrowing a particularly odious regime in one of the inhabited aspects, or generally fighting the good fight. All perfectly justifiable. Yes, he'd killed men, several. And quasi-men: nonhumans and not-quite-humans.

So, did he want more of that? Did he feel the overwhelming need to seek out such confrontations? To what purpose? Must he spill blood to set his own racing?

He stopped in front of another aspect, this one desiccated and bleak. He walked on.

No, he didn't like spilling blood. He was tired of conflict. The castle had gone through one convulsion after another in the past few years: siege, palace intrigue, dissension, invasion, and castlequake (extreme instability caused by stress and disharmony in the multiverse). He wanted a reprise of any of that? Absolutely not. The last thing he wanted was more *Sturm und Drang*.

Another portal, another world. There was not much out
there but salt flats under a deep purple sky. He continued
down the stone-lined corridor.

What he craved was adventure. He wanted to undertake
an expedition to discover something. Search for the source
of the Nile. Climb Everest. Sled through the Antarctic.
Plumb the depths of the Marianas Trench in a bathyscaphe.

Or find equivalents of any of those things in one of these
worlds.

Here was yet another aspect. And yet another picnic
ground. He thumbed through the printout, vainly trying to
find something of interest. He'd come to this floor because
a few of the descriptions sounded promising. He had failed
to locate any of the aspects described.

He flipped through page after page. Jeremy, the castle
data-processing chief, had given him the printout, but could
neither vouch for the data's accuracy nor warrant that it
wasn't completely obsolete. Aspects sometimes shifted
around, and this list had been compiled thousands of years
ago. Efforts were being made to update the records, but the
job was time-consuming.

Perhaps only Incarnadine, King of the Realms Perilous,
knew every aspect, where it was and what it was. However,
he claimed he didn't, and everyone usually took him at his
kingly word.

Gene lost his grip on the unwieldy printout and a section
of it dropped to the floor, trailing its paper tail. He stooped
to pick up the spill but in the doing dropped more. This
produced a blood-chilling oath. He kicked at the pile. Paper
all over the place.

He gathered up the whole mess and threw it into the
nearest alcove. Dusting his hands, he walked away.

He saw a room to his right and entered. It was one of the
castle's countless sitting rooms, furnished as usual with

dark carved chairs, a settee, and a few tables. Tapestries depicting hunting scenes draped the stone walls. This room seemed to get some use—there was a bowl of fresh fruit on one of the tables.

Gene shucked his backpack. He took an apple, lounged on the settee, and munched abstractedly.

This was useless. Either he wasn't being systematic enough or his luck had turned bad. Never before had he run into the problem of finding an interesting aspect. Used to be they popped up at the drop of a hat.

Maybe there was another problem. What used to be a novelty had long ago become commonplace. Maybe he'd seen enough interesting new worlds. Maybe he needed to go back home to his own.

But the longer he thought about going home, the less attractive the prospect seemed. Home? What was home? What was Earth, for that matter? One big heaving ball of storm and stress. He wondered what current world crisis was grabbing the headlines.

Not that he cared.

So, not going home left the alternative of staying here, which was boring. He wondered what in the world was wrong with him. Why could nothing in a fantastic enchanted castle captivate his imagination?

Could he be just plain depressed—clinically depressed? It happens to lots of people, he thought. Who granted you immunity?

But he didn't feel depressed, exactly; though what he was feeling—restlessness, boredom, and a sense that nothing really mattered—were suspicious symptoms. He gave some thought to the notion of seeking professional help.

Therapy? He was skeptical of its value. Something about all that shrink business had always struck him as questionable. Sure, therapy had it clinical uses, but for a person in generally good mental health to sit himself down . . .

Or was he just rationalizing? He considered his reluctance as a candidate for the symptom category.

Boy, they get you coming and going. Feel the need for therapy? No? Well, that simply means you need therapy.

He suddenly laughed.

You see, Doctor, I live in this big enchanted castle. And one day, while flensing a dragon, I suddenly got this overpowering feeling of futility. . . .

No, that would never do. They'd take him directly to the bouncy cubicle.

He sighed and tossed the half-eaten apple over his shoulder; then, regretting this act of thoughtlessness (the servants had enough work) he got up to retrieve it and saw that it had rolled through a doorway—an aspect, in fact— one that he had only half-noticed on entering.

Now he noticed it. This world was very nice, very nice indeed. He poked his head through. There was a clean, bracing wind blowing through a stand of pines to the right. Well, they looked like pines, but they were orange. On second thought they didn't look *much* like pine trees.

Even with orange non-pine trees, the terrain reminded him of places in Utah or western Colorado. Except for the colors: bright turquoise-blue rocks. Copper compounds? And a sort of pink sky. Airborne dust particles, he guessed.

Actually it didn't look a hell of a lot like anyplace he'd ever seen or visited. But it did look interesting. Sort of like photographs of a national park in Kodachrome-gone-mad.

He went back and fetched his gear. Wouldn't hurt to step through and look around. He wouldn't wander very far, not until he was sure this world was uninhabited. He could usually tell. Unpopulated worlds had a certain feel to them; and populated ones were sometimes all too unmistakable, especially those that succumbed to the temptations of technology (from stone axes to beverage cans). Litter was a trans-universal phenomenon.

He walked through the portal and out into a bright new world.

Yes, it was fairly obvious what he really wanted. Just a few days alone to ruminate and gather some wool. A little retreat to recharge the spiritual batteries. Had he really wanted adventure, he would have opted for an adventurous world, an inhabited one, a choice that would have necessitated research, reconnoitering, and extreme caution. To say nothing of breaching the language barrier, learning the customs, coming up with a convincing identity, and all that sort of undercover stuff. You couldn't really go traipsing into an inhabited aspect—or any aspect—without adequate preparation. He had violated that rule enough to know how dangerous it could be.

He really liked this world. Snow-hooded peaks to the north, as he reckoned north, an orange forest to the south—aquamarine badlands in between. Vegetation was strange not only in color. He passed a bush with diamond-like nodules depending from thin stalks. Another plant looked like an avant-garde sculpture constructed of clear plastic tubing.

He stopped to take a compass heading. His directional guesses were fairly true. The mountains lay to the magnetic north. He'd head toward them and try to find that crystal mountain lake. He probably wouldn't be able to eat the fish in the lake, though he had brought tackle and hand-line. This was hardly an Earth-like world, and the plant and animal proteins here probably didn't match his body chemistry. In other words, most everything that might appear edible would not be. He'd be living out of his backpack for a week. But that he was perfectly willing to do. He'd brought the best in freeze-dried comestibles.

The air was temperate, but it would likely get cold at night. That was no problem, however, as he had a high-tech wonder of a one-man tent and a mylar-lined sleeping bag that was rated down to minus 35 degrees Celsius.

He hiked along for about ten minutes, keeping the sun to his left as he threaded his way around upthrusting strata of greenish-blue. Yellow streaking ran through the rocks.

As he was coming down into a shallow canyon, a loud report shattered the air and made him jump. It was quite unexpected.

He looked up. No thunderclouds, and he was momentarily mystified until he saw the contrail of a fast-moving object in the sky. The noise had been a sonic boom.

"Oh, damn."

He'd have to head back. Despite his intuitions to the contrary, this world was not only inhabited but technologically sophisticated.

Nevertheless, for the moment he stayed, watching the thing make a harrowing high-g turn away from the sun and head back in his direction. It was an aircraft of some sort, and as it neared it looked rather like a small space shuttle. Silver-colored, compact and delta-winged, it was convincingly futuristic yet appeared eminently practicable.

But how was it going to set down? From his vantage point, Gene surveyed the available landing area. There wasn't nearly enough. Not unless the thing had vertical-landing capability.

The craft was floating along now, circling the canyon, staying airborne against all aerodynamic odds, when by rights it should have gone plunging groundward in a stall. Its flight path looked wobbly. After making a complete circuit of the canyon, the silvery vehicle began its approach for a landing. The only sound it made was the faint whoosh of air over its gracefully curving surfaces.

At the last second, the craft went out of control and hit the floor of the canyon hard—and flipped over. Gene dove behind a rock. But there was no explosion.

He got up, slapped his pants clean, and looked toward the crash site. The craft was silent and still except for a cloud of dust rising from the wreckage. Nothing else moved in the canyon. He jogged toward the downed craft.

As he neared, he slowed to a cautious walk. No telling who the survivors—if any—were. There was no way of knowing *what* they were, human or nonhuman, or how they would react. The plane said "human" to him, somehow, but that didn't make him any the less wary; it perhaps made him more so.

An oval hatch opened near the craft's blunt nose, dilating like an iris. A sigh of escaping air came to Gene's ears. He stopped. No one came out. He edged closer.

He peered into the interior. It was dark, and what was visible looked cramped and crowded with instrumentation. But there was room for him to enter, if he so decided.

He decided. He dropped his backpack and climbed through the hatch. Wires dangled in front of his face. He brushed them aside. Squeezing toward the nose, he walked gingerly over banks of instruments on the inverted overhead bulkhead.

Ahead, a human form hung upside down, snared in a tangle of straps, cables, and tubes. The pilot, he surmised, in a blue-and-silver pressure suit and transparent helmet. He got closer and bent over the still form.

It was a woman. And a very unusual-looking one. The hair, ghostly albino white, was cropped short. Her skin was suntan-dark, a Palm Beach mulatto. Her features were regular and broad, high cheekbones. Quite a striking face.

A beautiful one, once you got used to the contrasts. He put his face close to hers and peered through the helmet. Her eyelids opened slightly.

She was no albino. Her eyes were the darkest blue he had ever seen. They were purplish-blue besides, and he thought he detected flecks of green. He looked her over. There was a bloodied rip in her suit along the rib cage.

He didn't know quite what to do. He could not move her without risk of further serious injury; but he was reluctant to leave her hanging like this. She was obviously bleeding inside that suit. It would take at least twenty minutes to run back to the castle to get help, and a further twenty, minimum, before help arrived. He'd best get her down very gently, somehow, and then see what he could do to stabilize her with the first-aid stuff in the backpack. When he was sure she would last, he'd make a run to the castle.

He struggled out of the cabin, got the backpack, and went back inside, batting the same dangling wires out of the way. He went to her, knelt, and began unpacking.

Presently, he found the first-aid kit. He looked up and froze. He was staring into the business-end of a formidable-looking handgun.

Gene tilted his head to read her face. She was wide-eyed but not fearful. She looked angry. She said something in a language that sounded a cross between German and Latin, with a bit of Spanish thrown in for spice. When he didn't answer she spoke again, barking some kind of order.

"Sorry," he said finally. "I can't understand a word you're saying."

She scowled. Then her eyelids fluttered. The barrel of the gun dropped, as did her head to the deck. She relapsed into semiconsciousness.

Slowly, he reached for the weapon. She let go of it easily, and he exhaled and put the thing aside after giving it a glance and marveling. It looked like what a laser gun should look like.

He drew his knife and set himself to the task of untangling her. It was a rough job. He resorted to sawing at the hoses with his hunting knife. The straps were made of even tougher material, but he finally managed to clear her of those and had to react quickly when her legs dropped.

He eased her to the deck and straightened up, took a breath. It was hot inside and getter hotter. He worried about spilling fuel and the possibility of a sudden fire, and had a sudden flash of imagining what it would be like to be trapped inside.

He would have to risk moving her. She could move, and that meant her spinal cord was intact; he'd have to gamble that the spine itself wasn't broken.

He realized that her air supply had been interrupted and bent to the chore of getting her helmet off. There were fairly straightforward lugs on either side of the collar, and he undid these. He tried rotating the helmet clockwise, and when it wouldn't budge, tried the other way. It came of easily.

The fresh air seemed to bring her around.

She tried to get up, mumbling something.

"Can you walk?"

She grumbled something in reply.

"Let me help you."

He got her up. With difficulty, they struggled out of the craft. Outside, she collapsed to her knees, then sat with her head hung low.

He wanted to try something. He was no magician, like Linda and some few other castle Guests, but he could work a spell with a little luck. After you'd lived in the castle for a while, some of the magic rubbed off and stayed with you, even when you left the castle. Linda had taught him a trick that took advantage of this effect. It was a short incantation that invoked the castle's pervasive language-translation spell. Gene often used it when exploring inhabited aspects. Sometimes it worked for him, sometimes not. It was always worth a try.

He traced a circle in the air with his right index finger, made a cross over the circle, then uttered a one-syllable word.

He turned to her. "Are you all right?"

She looked up, surprised and suspicious. "You speak Universal. But you're an Outworlder."

"No. I'm using a . . . device."

"Implant?" He nodded. "You don't really look like an Outworlder. You look strange. What line are you of?"

"I come from a world you're probably not familiar with."

"What are you doing here? This planet is on the Preserve List. I must warn you that the Irregulars are on my trail. They may have guessed where I shunted off the Thread. I tried to randomize but they have ways of following a phased-photon trail. Something new they've come up with. If they find you with me, they'll kill you."

"What will they do to you?" he asked.

"Torture me. They'd do that no matter what." She took a deep breath, broke into a coughing fit, but eventually recovered. She looked Gene up and down. "Who are you?"

"Name's Gene. If you're in need of medical assistance, I can get help."

"Where?" She was genuinely puzzled. "Who is here on the planet?"

"It's kind of hard to explain. But I can get help if you need it."

"I will be fine," she said firmly. "I was thrown about during the attack, and my side—" She touched the rip in her pressure suit. "I bled some, but I think it's stopped. I don't think I sustained internal injury. Nothing serious, anyway."

"You'll need someone to see to that wound," Gene told her.

"You still haven't told me who you are and what you're doing here," she said pointedly. "Are you a freebooter? A privateer?"

"Sort of," Gene answered. "I—"

He was interrupted by more sonic booming. They looked up. Three white objects were etching wispy trails across the sky. Gene was sure now that the woman's craft was a spaceship—or at least a lifeboat of a larger spacecraft—and that these new arrivals were from space, too.

"They're here," she said flatly, no particular intonation to her voice except a weary casualness, as though death and danger were nothing out of the ordinary. She turned her head to Gene and smiled. "Would you be so kind as to fetch my pistol?"

Gene ducked back into the landing craft. When he came out he had both gun and backpack in hand. He gave the former to her.

"Thank you." She took it, checked it over, flipped a small lever on the breech, then handed it back. "Here."

He took the weapon. "What do you want me to do?"

"Again, if you would be so kind . . . shoot me."

PLANE

HE WALKED.

Above, a dark nothingness. Beneath his feet, an indeterminate hardness, neither stone nor dirt. More like an extrahard linoleum. Just a surface on which to tread.

There was a horizon, outlined by faint grayish light. It receded endlessly as he walked. He saw neither shadow nor substance. Not a rock or a rill. No geological complications of any sort. He strode across an infinite plane, vast and featureless.

He did not know who he was.

Rather, he suspected that he in fact did know who he was; it was simply a matter of that information being unavailable to him. Forgotten. For the moment. He was sure some part of him knew who he was.

Knowing that he knew gave him comfort. Otherwise he would have been lost. He kept reassuring himself that his loss of memory was only temporary, that it would return, and that once again he would be able to say his name. For he had quite forgotten it. But he knew he had a name.

Names were important. They bestowed identity. Identity;

precious commodity, that. In short supply, here on the Plane. For here A was not A. A was . . . it wasn't here. There existed only the Plane.

And himself, to be sure, and that was comfort as well. His own existence was reassuring. But without a name, existence was conditional. Discretionary. Contingent. Contingent upon . . . ?

He did not know. There was nothing.

His footsteps made no sound. He felt the fall of his feet through his bones. He had weight, mass, momentum (for after all, he moved), inertia (for sometimes he stopped), all the inherent physical quantities. He also had shape and color, though it was hard for him to perceive his color in the darkness. That was the sum total of what he knew about himself.

He liked walking. It gave him purpose. He had to have a purpose. There was nothing else for him to do. There was no direction here, so it was simply a matter of moving one's feet, a matter of shifting one's weight and balancing, shifting, balancing, again and again going through that sequence of shifts and balances that comprised the act of walking. No direction, for all directions were the same. He simply walked.

No direction, and no destination. There was no end to the Plane, no end to the walking of it. He would walk forever, and did not mind that so very much. It was good to walk, good to move.

But sometimes there must be a stopping, a resting.

He stopped. He turned.

The horizon was the same distance away as it had always been. Would always be. The same ghost-gray light illumined it, starkly, sharply, a razor-cut across the face of the darkness, yet somehow indeterminate. Infinite.

He looked down. The floor, the ground. Hardness. No

color to it. Dark. Gray, perhaps, but darkest gray. The gray of no color. Substance but no thingness. Hard, cold. This was a hard, cold place.

He sniffed, but smelled nothing. He seemed to have only a few senses, not the full complement. He could see. He could feel, somewhat. He could not hear, he could not smell. Perhaps he did and there was nothing to hear or smell. It mattered little which case obtained. It was the same either way.

He resumed walking. He wondered if he was breathing. It did not seem to him that he was. He felt no air, no wind. He tried to breathe. And succeeded. But did he need to breathe? Was he actually drawing air into his lungs? Indeed, did he have lungs, need lungs?

He had no idea. There was much he did not know. Correction. Much that he had forgotten. For a man never ceases knowing who and what he is. But he does sometimes forget.

He stopped again. Had he heard something?

He turned once completely around. Nothing.

There was nothing to hear. He moved on.

He asked himself where he might have been before he came to this place. He had no answer. What had he been doing just prior to his arrival here? No answer.

He considered the question of time. He came to a conclusion. There was no time here, either. He had always been here.

No! Something in him rejected that. He had not always been here. Therefore, there had been a beginning of his being here. He could not place it in time, but there had been an arrival here, a beginning of this walking. There was time, after all. It was just that there was so little to mark its passing.

Again, he thought he had heard something. He stopped

and listened intently. He thought he had heard the calling of a name. Distant, very distant.

His name? But how would he know his name?

He wished his name would return to him. Perhaps if he heard, clearly, distinctly, he would recognize it for what it was. But he could hear nothing now. He doubted that there was anything to hear. He had imagined it, wishing for it so mightily.

He began walking again. He maintained the same pace as before. A brisk walk, a purposeful walk. He had nowhere to go, nothing to do when he got there. No direction, no destination.

What kind of world was it, he wondered, in which there was so little? So very little. Darkness, hardness, a bit of light . . . himself . . . and that was all. What kind of universe was that? How could it exist? Who could dream of such a place? For there was nothing to dream of. It was . . . a fever dream. A fever dream of a place. (He could barely remember what fever was. He wasn't quite sure.) But whose fever? Whose dream?

His. His dream. He was dreaming. But it was not like a dream. It was too much like being awake to be a dream. (He could not remember, exactly, what a dream was.) Yet it had to be a dream.

His thinking was not very clear. That he knew. Better to avoid thinking too much. Thinking led to confusion. It was enough to walk. To move, though he moved in a direction-less space, along an infinite plane.

He returned to the question of what he did before he came to this place. He had done something. He had had a life. Of that he was sure.

Life. That was a strange concept. Life struck him as something exciting, interesting, infinitely varied. Fluid. Not like this, which was unchanging and absolute. Life was not like this. Life was change, constant change. There was no change here. Life was movement with a purpose, a goal, a motive. None of those qualities was present in the circumstances in which he now found himself. Life was . . . much more than this. That was about all he could say on the matter, though. He did not remember his life. All he knew was that it had been quite different from the existence he led now.

When had the transition between life and this existence occurred? What had occasioned it?

There were too many questions and too few means at his disposal to begin to answer them. Again, he told himself that it was best not to think.

But he had to think. It was his nature to think.

Ah! So he did know something about his nature after all! He was a thinker. He thought. He had been thinking all along, his mind racing like a machine with its gears disengaged, wheels spinning, revolving in their cycles. But to what purpose was all that thinking? None that he could divine.

He kept walking. He wanted to walk. He would keep doing it, for it was his only function in this world. His necessary and sufficient cause for being.

The horizon was far, just as far as it always had been, always would be. He would walk forever, the darkness hanging over him, an infinite band of gray spectral light encompassing him, a horizon delimiting the limitlessness of his world.

It was enough.

Sea

THE SEA WAS PLACID, the sky hazy. Not a good day for sailing. There was a breeze but it barely stirred the jib. No trace of a whitecap in sight. The surface was like tepid water left standing inside a bathtub. A tropical inversion had settled in, becalming everything adrift.

Trent gave up. He dropped anchor, though there was no need. The sloop *Inside Straight* was dead in the water.

The sun had tanned him, bleaching his butter-colored hair to cornsilk white, and the wind and weather had turned his handsomeness rugged. He had done a lot of sailing lately, living in this aspect, Sheila's world.

Sheila, his wife.

She, of the red hair and wild magical talent, was stretched out prone on the deck, sunbathing in the nude.

One arm resting on the mainsail boom, he admired the shapeliness of her posterior, appreciating its perfect hemispherical geometry. He also deeply approved of the long legs, the ample thighs, the well-turned calves, the perfect, arched feet. There were three brown freckles on her broad oiled back, and he liked those as well.

"You're going to burn," he said.

"I have super sun-blocker on."

"You always burn. You turn into lobster thermidor within five minutes."

Scowling, she turned over and sat up. "Isn't it the truth. Redheads never tan, damn it anyway." She ran a hand over her left arm. "I hate my complexion."

"Don't you dare."

"It's mine. I get to hate it if I want."

"I like what it's wrapped around."

She smiled. "Come here and kiss me, sailor."

He went to her and did.

She bit his nose. "You're so damned good-looking, I could eat you."

"Sounds great."

"I like the cut of your jib, sailor."

"And my mainsail?"

"Your what?"

He pointed.

She looked. "Oh. That, too."

"You just like nautical men."

"Naughty men. The naughtier the better."

"You're taking quite a chance saying that, dressed the way you are."

"I'm not dressed at all, dear."

"*Au contraire*, in your finest."

"Thank you, dear." She kissed him again. "Hot, isn't it?"

He took off his mirrored sunglasses and rubbed his eyes. "Aye, that it is. And muggy. We'll probably have to use the motor to get home."

"No wind, huh?"

"We are becalmed. If we wait an hour or two, the heat will rise and cooler air will come, on a breeze. But I don't feel like lying to for that long. Besides, this is squall weather."

"Maybe a good storm will cool things off."

"It might cool us off—permanently, if we get stuck out here in it."

"I trust you implicitly, Captain. You'll get us safely back to Sheila's Cove."

"And SheilaWorld."

" 'Club Sheila,' please. Trent?"

"Yes, my dear?"

"Have you enjoyed our living here?"

"Of course."

"You're not bored, helping me run this little resort?"

"As a career, resort-hotel management offers many chances for advancement and personal fulfillment."

She whacked him on the shoulder. "Seriously. Have you minded awfully much?"

"Not at all, my dear. It's a wonderful place. Sun, sand, sea, and great banana daiquiris."

"You don't get bored sometimes?"

"Oh, maybe a little. And a bit annoyed, when we get a particularly fussy guest."

"You mean like Lord Peter."

"Ever since Incarnadine made the error of elevating him to the peerage, he's been insufferable."

"Wasn't he an aristocrat or something before? I mean, back in England? He always acted like it."

"I doubt it. But I'm sure he always thought that was an oversight that should be corrected. And now, thanks to Inky . . ."

" 'His Majesty,' please."

"Oh, to hell with him."

"Trent! He's the king!"

"He's my brother, and I love him. Like a brother. Would you like some champagne, my dear?"

"Do I ever refuse?"

Trent got up and fetched the cooler. Soon, a cork popped and flew on an arching trajectory into the sea.

Sheila yelled, "Pollution!"

"It's our world; we can pollute it a little, as we're its only inhabitants."

"What an attitude!" Sheila said reprovingly. "All the more reason to keep it pure."

"A bit of cork is not pollution. Be quiet and drink this."

"Yes, my lord. Thank you. Nice champagne glasses. Where'd you . . . not from the bar, I hope?"

"Where else?"

"We're running short of glassware."

"You'll conjure more."

"It's hard work! Really, I can't keep up with the maintenance of this place. Light bulbs, dishes, towels—"

"Why the hell do people steal towels from hotels?" Trent mused. "I've always been mystified by that."

"And ashtrays! And soap, and sugar bowls, and anything else that's not nailed down."

"Comes with the territory. What I want to know is who these 'people' are who are hotel guests and who aren't from the castle."

"They came with the hotel when I conjured it," Sheila said.

"Phantasms."

"Window dressing."

"Props," he said. "Lifeless props."

"I've talked to a few. They're nice people."

Trent sipped his champagne. "One of these days you'll have no other choice than to consign them all to the oblivion whence they came. When you finally get tired of this little island paradise you created."

"Think I'll get tired of it?"

"Do *you* think you will?"

Sheila mulled it over. "I like it here much better than the castle. The castle's dark and gloomy."

"Castles tend to be that way."

"Especially Perilous."

"Well, yes. But it has one hundred forty-three thousand nine hundred ninety-nine more game rooms besides this one."

"Some of them are downright creepy."

"Oh, sure, but some are quite delightful. I wouldn't mind a change of scenery."

"Really? Trent, do you want to move?"

"No, dear. I want to be where you are happiest. And I think that, for the moment, you are happiest here." Trent crossed his legs and sipped thoughtfully. "But paradise can be ultimately boring. I do miss the castle every once in a great while."

Sheila set down her glass and stretched out again, this time on her back. "I thought you said you can't ever live at Perilous. Because of the curse?"

"Well, it's a mild curse."

"Your father put it on you, right?"

"Yep. Old Dad. The king."

"You've never really explained why."

"Well, simply put, Dad banished me from the castle because I was a rotten kid."

"Were you a rotten kid?"

"I was young. And hot-headed. And ambitious. I wanted to be king."

"But your dad favored Incarnadine over you."

"For the succession, yes."

"Incarnadine is older than you, isn't he?"

"No," Trent answered. "I am. By four minutes."

Sheila's head popped up. "What?"

"We're twins. Fraternal twins."

"You never told me that."

Trent considered it. "No, I don't believe I ever did. It's true, though."

"This four-minute difference—is that why you thought you should be king? Some legal thing?"

"Dad didn't care a fig about legalities. Dad liked Inky a lot. He hated me. There was no question in his mind who should wear the crown after he died."

"And Inky . . . I mean, Incarnadine, was crowned when that happened."

"Yes, but not until after I gave him a run for his money."

"I've heard stories about how you challenged him."

"Mostly blown out of proportion. But I'll have to admit I got rather insistent about it." Trent stretched out his legs and leaned back against the bulkhead. He chuckled. "Do you know how long ago that was?"

"I know you two are getting along in years," Sheila said, "for all that you both still don't look a day over thirty-five."

"Magic, my dear. Magic."

"Great stuff, magic. So, about this curse. You can't set foot in the castle?"

"Oh, I can set foot in it, all right. But I can't stay for long. Eventually I get an overpowering urge to leave."

"Too bad."

"It used to be worse. Used to be I'd get anxiety attacks. The shakes. I've done some work against the spell over the years to reduce its effectiveness."

Sheila asked, "Are you saying you could live in the castle now?"

"I'm really not sure. The spell may have lost potency on its own. Spells do that, with time."

A gull screeched somewhere off in the lazy silence.

Trent looked up at the canopy of fuzzy, blue-dyed cotton that was the sky. "I honestly don't know if I could stay in the castle for any length of time. But I'm fairly sure I'm not interested in trying."

"Then we'll stay here for the time being?"

"As I said, Sheila, dear—where you're happiest is where I want to be."

"You're so gallant. So damned gallant."

"I'm a prince, hey."

"A prince of a prince."

"And you're a princess, don't forget. A princess of the Realms Perilous."

Sheila sat up and pulled her husband close. She kissed him. "Thanks for making my life a fairy tale."

"My pleasure. You know, when I first met you, I—"

Trent suddenly turned his head shoreward.

"We have company," he said.

Sheila got to her knees and looked. "The speedboat. Snowy's probably waterskiing again."

"Look again. It's the speedboat all right, but no skiers. Heading right for us."

"Something must have happened at the hotel," Sheila said with concern, reaching for the two scraps of cloth that were her bikini. "That must be Julio piloting."

"It's not Julio," Trent said, shielding his eyes. "This is interesting."

"Who is it?"

"Looks like Tyrene, a couple of Guardsmen with him."

"What? They never come here!"

"No." Trent's brow lowered.

"Trent, what do you think is up?"

"We'll soon find out." Trent got to his feet.

The speedboat cut its engines and turned, its starboard aligning with the sailboat's port. One of the Guardsmen stood and threw a line.

Tyrene, Captain of the Castle Guard, waved and shouted, "Ahoy!"

Trent caught the line, tied the end off. The Guardsman hauled the two craft close enough to bump gently against each other.

"Your Royal Highness," Tyrene said, "if you'll pardon the intrusion . . ."

"What's up, Tyrene?"

"Permission to come aboard, sir?"

"Permission granted."

It took some doing. Tyrene was the lubbiest of landlubbers. Trent helped him onto the deck of the sloop, where he eventually spilled.

Trent had immediately taken ominous readings from Tyrene's grave expression, but said casually, "Something's up at the castle, I take it."

Tyrene came to unsteady attention. "Your Royal Highness, a disaster of unprecedented magnitude has befallen us. I regret to inform you that your brother, the king, is dead."

A gasp escaped Sheila's lips before both hands shot up to cover her mouth.

Trent turned his head and stared out to sea. A long interlude followed, the only sound that of wavelets lapping at Fiberglas hulls.

At last Trent looked back. "How?"

"He was found dead this morning, at his desk, locked within his quarters at the Elector's palace."

"In . . . ?"

"Malnovia. That is the aspect, sir. He was Court Magician there."

"Malnovia, Malnovia." Trent scratched his bare chest. "I recall the name but can't put any images with it."

"The milieu is not unlike Earth, western Europe, eighteenth century, sir. Highly developed science, but largely agrarian . . ."

"Yeah, I remember. Fine music, just like Earth's in that period, only slightly different harmonic conventions and freer musical forms . . ." Trent exhaled. "Now, why do I remember trivialities like that?"

"Sir, His Majesty was fond of the aspect chiefly for its music."

Trent nodded. "Inky's a classicist through and through." He looked out to sea again. "*Was*. But you haven't told me how he died."

"Sir, I regret to say that the cause is not yet known. However, the court physician was summoned and he pronounced the king dead. Later, our Dr. Mirabilis confirmed. Your Royal Highness, I am afraid there is no doubt about it. The king is dead."

"Long live the king," Trent intoned. "But I regret to say I have forgotten his name."

"The king's only son and heir is Brandon."

"Ah, Brandon. Yes, of course. Fine lad. How old?"

"Twelve, sir."

"Seems he was born last Tuesday." Trent inhaled salt air deeply, let it out. "So."

"There is the matter of appointing his regent, sir."

"The ministers have met?"

"Not yet, sir. They will do so within the hour. I was instructed to beg the honor of your presence as they discuss this gravest of issues."

Trent nodded. "Please inform the ministers of the Privy Council that I will be in Council Chambers within the hour." Trent wet a finger and held it up. "That is to say, if we get half a breeze out here."

"Sir, if I might make a suggestion—"

Trent glanced at the speedboat. "No, we'll stay with the *Inside Straight*. I don't trust your men to bring her in safely, even under power. They don't have a nautical look about them."

Tyrene straightened up. "But, Your Royal Highness—"

"I need time to clear my wits, Tyrene. I may be a little late, but I'll be there. Tell them not to start without me."

Tyrene slumped. "Yes, sir."

"Buck up, old man. These things are inevitable, even with the long life-spans the likes of us are blessed with."

"I suppose. Nevertheless . . ." Tyrene groped for words.

"Yes, a death's a shock to the system. All the more so for the false sense of security we're lulled into because of its long postponement."

"Aye." Tyrene sighed and looked off forlornly. "He was a great man."

Trent hesitated the barest second. "One of the greatest. Now, off with you. This is a vulnerable time, a critical juncture if there ever was one. You're needed back at Perilous."

"Aye." Tyrene came to attention once again. "Your Royal Highness." He turned slightly and bowed. "My lady."

"Oh, Tyrene." Sheila went to him and hugged him.

Tyrene looked uncomfortable hugging back.

"I must go, my lady."

"Be careful."

And he tried to be. But in the attempt to reboard the launch, his rubbery land-legs failed him. He got caught with one foot in each perversely drifting boat, and for some reason neither his men nor Trent could prevent him from falling into the drink with a mighty splash. He got a full ducking, head to toe.

No one laughed. They hauled him out.

Miserable beyond human endurance, Tyrene nevertheless bore up with dignity. "It hasn't been a good day," he said.

Trent cast them off. The motor came to life, and the launch sped away, heading back to the marina. The small sloop bobbed in its wake.

Sheila looked stricken. "I can't believe it. I just can't believe he's dead."

After a moment Trent said, "Neither can I."

They hugged each other a good while before making preparations for getting the vessel underway.

Trent went below and fiddled with the emergency engine until it coughed and began chugging merrily.

As soon as it did, a sailor's mistress of a sea breeze came across the water to luff the sails.

PLANET

THEY STUMBLED through forests of boulders, following a twisting path. She could walk, but the pain in her side was excruciating, or so Gene guessed from her constant grimacing and lip-biting. He helped her along while glancing constantly skyward, expecting strange, hostile spacecraft to appear at any second.

But whoever was in pursuit seemed to have lost the scent. Gene guessed that the three craft he had seen streaking through the planet's upper atmosphere had either overshot their intended landing site or were deploying into a wide search pattern.

He asked, "Do you think their instruments got a fix on you as you landed . . . uh, crashed?"

"They were tracking me as I deorbited, but I employed . . ." She grunted as she stepped up to a ledge. "I used every deception ploy and decoy device that the lander had to offer. Something might have worked."

"Seems to have."

"They'll be following phantom sensor readings for a

good while. We may have time enough to reach the test mine—if we're lucky."

"Test mine?"

"Yes, a test shaft and a number of tunnels, if the information I have is correct. Production mining never commenced here, and the facility was mothballed. Unless scavengers found it, there may be an operating multiphone there."

"Some kind of radio?"

She gave him a curious look. "What strange terminology you use. Radio? No. It doesn't broadcast on the usual spectra. It employs paired virtual photons to propagate probability waves through . . ." She shrugged. "You must be a bumpkin from the darkest of galactic provinces if you need the principles of superluminal* communication explained to you."

"Yeah, you might say I'm from the boondocks," Gene told her.

She frowned. "Could it be that you don't speak Universal? I seem to be understanding you, but I just suddenly realized you're actually speaking some other tongue. Do you have a running translator working?"

"Sort of."

"It must be very sophisticated. You had me fooled."

"It is sophisticated, very," Gene said. "It's downright magical, in fact. How far to this mine thing?"

"It should be just over this next ridge. Uhhh . . ."

She sank to her knees.

"Take it easy. Do you want to rest?"

"No!" She forced herself to rise as he assisted. "We must get there and send for help. It's only a matter of time before they realize they've been fooled and begin to recognize our life readings hidden in the false data."

*Faster than light.

They moved on. The pink sky looked darkly ominous now, as if warning of a strange storm to come. The orange scrub moved nervously with the breeze. The rocks looked greener here, shading from verdigris to jade.

They made their way across rugged terrain for a good ten minutes.

"Kind of obvious question, and maybe I'm missing something," Gene said, "but won't your broadcast on this multiphone gadget—By the way, it is a broadcast you're talking about, something that can be detected easily?"

"A multiphone transmission can be detected by anyone with a multiphone receiver anywhere in the universe."

"I see. So my question is, Won't your transmission give our position away?"

"Not at all." She was out of breath. "No way to . . . determine the origin of a multiphone transmission . . . omnidirectional . . . uhhh."

"We've got to slow down. You could be bleeding again."

She suddenly pointed. "There!"

Gene looked ahead. An inverted hexagonal umbrella, looking very like an advanced communications dish, was jutting above the crest of the next hill.

"Isn't this the first place they'll look?" he asked.

"Not if the lander's decoy drones succeed in convincing the Irregulars that I came down on the other side of the planet," she said. "They won't search here until they realize they've been hoodwinked."

"Another obvious question," Gene said as he helped her up the steep rise. "Why do they want you?"

She was silent.

"Just thought I'd ask," he said.

"How do I know you're not an Irregular agent?"

"Would I be helping you?"

"You could be leading me into a trap while trying to get

me to divulge information without resorting to either torture
or mind probe. Not that either would yield anything of
value."

"I concede the point."

She gave him an analytical look. "But I don't think you
are an Irregular. You're a bit of mystery. You haven't even
mentioned your ship. If you have one, *that* is the first place
they would have looked—unless your ship is in a stealth
mode that is beyond their capacities to defeat. In which
case, you might just be a freebooter."

He said, "In which case I might be tempted to turn you
over to your pursuers for any reward they might offer. Are
they offering a reward?"

"None that I know of," she replied. "The Supreme
Command of the Irregular Forces of the Liberation would
probably thank you for contributing to the cause of bringing
down the central government of the Dominion of Worlds.
And then they would likely kill you to cover up any traces
of their actions here."

"Oh."

"But you are free to take the gamble that they might just
impress you into service. They do that, you know."

"I'm not impressed," Gene said. "But don't worry, I'm
not about to meddle in affairs I know nothing about. All I
know is that you're hurt, you're in trouble, and you're the
shapeliest shuttle pilot I've ever seen. I just want to prevent
further harm from befalling you."

"You are a strange one. Where *is* your ship?"

"Don't have one, sorry."

"Then . . ." She fell silent as they neared the tall
silo-shaped building, prickly with numerous antennae, that
stood on the slope of the next hill. Behind it stood other
functional structures. The silo was buff-colored with a

yellow door at its base. The door's only feature was a square shiny plate.

She slumped to the ground in front of the door, exhausted. Gene bent to inspect the plate.

"Some kind of electronic lock, I guess."

When she caught her breath she said, "No doubt the security system has already scanned us and decided we're unlikely candidates for admission."

"How did you plan on getting in?"

She unzipped a pouch on her pressure suit and withdrew a small black box with dials and readouts on it. "This." She fiddled with the settings, then handed it to him.

He took it and examined it. The markings were indecipherable, but somehow he tumbled to the thing's function. There was an adhesive strip on the back.

"Timed charge?"

She nodded. "It's powerful enough to take out the side of the building, so it must be set back a distance. Put it about . . ." She sized up the building. "Here." She pointed.

He walked to the spot. "Right here?"

"Yes. But—"

"What?"

"There is one flaw to my plan," she said glumly, "such as it is. They'll readily detect any major energy discharge."

"Now, that's a problem."

"Yes." She crossed her legs and let out a breath. "I didn't have much time to think this through. But I suppose the only thing to do is rush for the communications room and get off the transmission as quickly as possible. After that the only thing we can do is hide in one of the tunnels."

"Where they'd have us neatly cornered."

"True." Her purplish-blue eyes rolled. "I suppose it's useless."

"Don't give up yet."

Gene approached the door and eyed it up and down.

"Do you have any ideas?" she asked.

"This security system you mentioned, the way you phrased it—" He ran a hand over the smooth yellow-painted metal of the door. "Is it controlled by an Artificial Intelligence?"

"Of course," she said. "How else could a security system know friend from foe?"

"Right. If we did get in, we'd have to contend with it. True?"

"We'd have to take it out."

"Hmm. First we have to get in. I'm going to try something."

"What?"

"Little magic trick I know."

Gene squared himself in front of the door and extended his right hand, bringing the palm up flush with the metal plate.

She watched with interest.

" 'Cottleston, Cottleston, Cottleston pie,' " he began.

She was very interested. One pale eyebrow rose.

" 'A fly can't bird but a bird can fly,' " he finished.*

He repeated the couplet several times, keeping perfectly still, fixing his gaze straight ahead.

Presently the door emitted a high-pitched tone. It emitted several more in a complex harmonic sequence, then beeped dissonantly. After a few more seconds it slid aside with a hiss.

"Amazing," she said.

"Nothing to it."

"Whatever was that?"

*See *Winnie-the-Pooh* by A. A. Milne.

"A little facilitation spell. I can't do much in the way of hocus-pocus, but I can do a door-opener in worlds with manageable indigenous magic. Fortunately, this is such a world."

She guffawed. "You're a magician?"

"An inept one. Please, I'm very sensitive about it."

She laughed.

"Don't you have any compassion for the handicapped?"

"I have no idea who you are or what you're up to," she said, "but you do have style, that much I'll say."

"Style is the last refuge," he replied as he helped her up, "of those who are short in the substance department."

The strange building was dark inside. They entered cautiously.

PLANE

THE HORIZON HAD LIGHTENED a bit, he thought. But he could not be sure. He had been walking for . . . how long? But there was no time, of course. Nothing, except . . .

Was it that he had a better conception of himself? Not a conception, exactly. It might best be said that he had a firmer grasp on his own reality. The situation had been touch and go for a while. (Timelike words again! No avoiding them, try as he might.) He had felt that he would dissolve, fade away. But now he was fairly sure that his existence, such as it was, would continue for an indefinite time into an indeterminate future. That was something. Not much, but something.

There was not much else, however. His name still eluded him. He had no memories to speak of. Only, now, a vague sense that much had gone on before.

Well, that was more than he had possessed on his arrival here. . . .

Again, the persistence of time. Perhaps time did have a meaning here. Things were changing, albeit imperceptibly. Conditions were . . . improving. No. That was exaggeration. It was enough that things were changing, and perhaps changing in an important way.

But on the other hand . . .

Did he have two hands? He looked at them. Yes.

But on the other hand, not much about this place had changed. It was barely a place at all. There was a nothingness about it that was disquieting, that defeated him. There was too much nothingness here. In fact, there was almost no "here" in which to contain a nothingness. There was absolutely nothing to distinguish any one point on this plane from any other . . .

Until now.

He stopped. Far ahead, something rose above the horizon. It wasn't much of anything but a line, a spike, a rise of something that had no characteristics save that it was perpendicular to the line of the horizon. It seemed very far away.

A goal! He had a goal! He strode forward eagerly.

Unlike the horizon, this new feature of the universe got closer the more one walked toward it. As he neared, it got bigger, and he began to notice that it was thicker at its base. It was a tall, thin pyramid—an obelisk, and there was something at the top, an irregular shape, but he still could not distinguish it.

He hurried toward it.

He arrived at the column's base and found that he could barely see the top. It was almost lost in the darkness. Yet he could make out a shape.

It looked like a man up there. Yes, very definitely, though the features were indiscernible. The man seemed to be sitting atop the obelisk, seated in a wing chair. The chair rested on a capital that crowned the shaft.

He stared up at the figure. It did not move. He continued watching. Before long he could have sworn that he detected movement, perhaps a slight shifting of the figure. But no more than that. Whatever or whoever it was preferred not to move.

But as time (yes!) passed he began to see that there was more to the figure, and became convinced that the small platform at the apex of the obelisk held more than just the figure and the seat. The figure . . . yes, it was a man, a man dressed in a long gown and a pointed cap . . . was bent over a small writing desk or lectern. He was writing, slowly and methodically, with a quill in a large ledger, his attention to detail fastidious, the tip of the quill precessing equinoctially, in slow circles.*

Time passed.

Below, the one who looked up waited. He stood completely still, eyes on the figure above. Waiting. Waiting.

A further duration ran its course. At some point in a moving stream of time that was now well-established, a few moments later or several hours later—no one could say— the man on high laid the quill aside and settled within the wings of his high-backed chair.

Something had changed in the interim. The obelisk was not so much an obelisk as a high bench—a very high bench, such as that from which a judge might deliberate.

The man in the gown and pointed cap looked down. The face was vague in shadows, but a flowing beard could be discerned, its color perhaps a silver-gray. The eyes, under a dark lowered brow, were pools of deeper shadow.

He spoke. He said, "Ah." His voice was deep and resonant.

---

*The precession of the equinoxes is the earlier occurrence of the equinoxes in each successive sidereal year because of a slow retrograde motion of the equinoctial points along the ecliptic, caused by the wobble inherent in the Earth's rotation, much like that of a spinning top.

The man below said nothing.

The Judge (for after all, he must have a name) glanced at the open book. "I was just working on your entry. Good. You have come. Your time has come. Rather, the end of your time. There now must be a reckoning."

More time passed, enough so that the man below felt he must answer.

"Where am I?"

The Judge smiled faintly. "Where, indeed. If this is a place, it is a place between places. Less a place than a transition between places. Between different states of being, shall we say. The notion of physical location is moot. This is not so much a place as it is a way station. A short stop on the journey."

"On the journey to where?"

"That is what must be determined."

"If you can't tell me where I am," the man below said, "then tell me who I am."

"*That* also must be determined. Identity is not a constant thing. It shifts. It flows. It must be stabilized. It needs bolstering now and then. Reinforcing. It is not a given."

The man below stared at the ground for a moment. Then he looked up again. "What am I doing here? Why was I brought to this place?"

"You are full of questions," the Judge said. He smiled again and nodded. "Good. You must regard what is happening to you as a process, a situation in a state of becoming. You must ask questions, you must learn. You must forget what you know, or what you think you know, and you must learn it again, afresh. With the relearning might come something new. New knowledge. Sharper insight. A change of perspective. And all that will come, in time. You must learn, as well, to be patient."

"I want to know," the man below said. "I want to learn."

"Good, good. You will learn. And you will know."

The Judge leaned back and rubbed his eyes with thumb and forefinger. "Ah," he said wearily. "This is not the easiest of jobs."

"Who are you?" the man looking up asked.

"It is my job to see you through this process of learning. To guide you, but not to teach. You must teach yourself. I will be with you in spirit along the way. It is also my appointed task to choose a proper path for you. There are many paths to knowledge. Many means to the ultimate goal. One way must be chosen that is right for you, that is more conducive to self-instruction than any other."

"Where am I to go?" was the question.

"Do not ask where," came the answer. "As I told you, location is of little importance. More significant is the process itself. Forget for now the question of where in space and time the process unfolds. For your purposes, there is no space, save for that space in which you are to fulfill your destiny. There is no time, save for the duration needed for that destiny to be fulfilled."

"Is it all written?" asked the man. "Is it all set down in that book?"

The Judge nodded, leaning forward again, looking over the edge of the towering bench. "I am writing it. It is being written even as we speak."

"Then I have no will, no volition."

"On the contrary! You have every means at your disposal to change the circumstances in which you will find yourself. You will have the wherewithal to resist, to fight, to scheme, to meddle, or to refuse. All is possible. All this you will do."

"But if my fate is sealed . . ."

"In eternity, your fate is set. But you live in time, and you have the means and the opportunity to affect the outcome of all that you engage in. You will choose your fate. You will cause it to be fixed in eternity. You will be the only cause of your own predetermined fate. You will write your story. And I . . . I will set it down. Here." The Judge touched the pages of the open ledger.

The man did not answer for a long while. The silence of the Plane droned on.

"I find all that . . . very interesting."

"No doubt," the Judge said. He sat back again. "There is not much more to say. Words, at this point, would be of little value."

"You have not said many," the man below said. "Nor have you told me very much."

"That is true. For many reasons. And you will know the reason in time, as you shall know many things."

The Judge straightened in his chair.

"It is time to begin."

"Begin what?"

The horizon, the man suddenly noticed, was barely visible now, a faint ring of grayness that had slowly faded as the conversation progressed. The darkness that was not a sky above seemed to grow darker still. Shadows fell upon one another across the length and breadth of the Plane. Silence deepened.

"What is happening?"

"Nothing," the Judge said. "This temporary existence is at an end. Chaos returns, darkness falls."

"Will something take its place?"

"Perhaps. Perhaps not."

"What is written in the book about it?"

"Only what you create and I set down."

"But what does the book say?"

"If I read, it would be meaningless to you."

The darkness folded in like a shroud. The horizon

became the barest ghost of itself, a thin separation of the blackness above and the blackness below. Then it vanished and there was naught but the absence of light.

"This is meaningless," he said in the last moment before he ceased to exist.

"What is?" came the last thing he heard.

CHAMBER OF THE PRIVY COUNCIL

THEY WERE ALL ELDERLY MEN, all sitting around an immense oak table.

Dressed in fine robes and bedecked with heavy gold chains from which hung ornate gold medallions—signifying their respective offices and posts—they sat, hatted or hooded, in wary silence, eyes shifting, each taking his neighbor's measure.

Mental wheels turned, spinning out plots and counter-plots, assessing possible allies, gauging potential enemies. On the surface, there were a few bland smiles. The majority wore poker faces. Most went about their machinations calmly, coolly; one or two looked nervous.

One stroked his white beard, face forward, eyes sidling left. The man next to him met his gaze, raised an eyebrow. The first man looked away.

Someone coughed discreetly into a bony fist.

Points of candlelight glinted in dark oak paneling, richly stained and finished. It was a subdued room. A room of power. The chairs were of black crushed leather, the candlesticks of gold. The bare tabletop shone with a waxen luster.

Now and then, eyes drifted to the large empty chair at the end of the table farthest from the door.

Someone else coughed. More looks were exchanged— silent offers and counteroffers; implied claims; tacit demurrals.

Presently one of them began, "Well, I should think—"

He was interrupted by the sound of the chamber doors creaking open. A page entered and stood to one side, at attention.

"His Royal Highness, Trent, Prince of the Realms Perilous!"

Trent strode in, green cape billowing.

All rose.

"Good day, my lords."

Greetings in turn were murmured around the Council table.

All eyes were on him as he walked around the table. All took note of the resplendent finery: the silks, the ermines, the chased sword hilt in its jewel-encrusted scabbard, the sparkling gems on almost every finger. The hat was black with green trim, an enormous white plume sprouting from it.

Trent reached his place at the head of the table.

"Be seated, good my lords."

They waited till he took his seat. Then they sat. The page retreated, the doors of the chamber closed. A hushed quiet fell.

Trent looked energetically confident and completely self-sufficient. His gaze was a withering beam that swept the table. His head swiveled only slightly. He looked from side to side, back and forth, once, twice, thrice, raking the solemn array of powerful men.

Then he smiled.

"It seems we have a problem."

A minister to Trent's left rose. He bowed. "Your Royal Highness. I think I speak for all my colleagues in expressing our sincerest condolences in this, your family's hour of grief. Rest assured that we all share the pain of this most devastating and inconsolable loss, the loss not only of your dear brother, but of our liege lord and king."

Trent nodded. "Thank you, Lord Burrel. And on behalf of my family, let me say that I feel secure in the knowledge that the day-to-day handling of the affairs of state will be in competent hands during this difficult period of change and transition. You have our every confidence and faith."

Burrel bowed again. "Your Highness, my colleagues and I are ever your humble and obedient servants."

"Fine," Trent said. "Now let's get to business. We have a boy king. A boy king wants a regent. I'm here to present the case for my taking on the job."

Burrel slowly sat as a collective exhalation went up from the table. They had all known it was coming.

Another minister rose. "Sir, if I may be permitted to speak—?"

"Please, Lord Tragg."

"I think it safe to say that Council will entertain any proposition or proposal that His Highness might wish to advance, and will, in due course, render its decision. But I beg His Highness to bear in mind that many and various considerations will be weighed in the balance before any settlement might be reached on so critical a matter as this. Such a process takes time."

Trent shook his head. "No, Lord Tragg, the Realms cannot wait. We need a king, a ruler. We have one in the person of a twelve-year-old boy, a fine boy who will one day, no doubt, make a splendid king, given the proper

education and training. My lords, I fully expect that
Brandon will in due course take the throne and reign, and,
if he's any son of his father, there is every chance that he'll
rule with a will. But that day is distant. What do we do in
the meantime? There are one hundred forty-four thousand
worlds to be looked after. There are a thousand worlds to
govern directly, thousands more we have a hand in ruling,
either through our proxies, puppets, and dupes, or through
other covert means. How is all this to be done in the
interim?"

"Your Highness," Tragg said, "we have not yet come to
a decision. The king is not yet three hours dead—that is to
say, it has been less than that time since his body was
discovered. Surely you don't think we can—"

"The decision must be made immediately," Trent said.

"Impossible, Your Highness," spoke the man to Tragg's
right. "As Lord Tragg said, many deliberations must be
made. There are many factors to be brought into the
calculations. These things must be approached with some
delicacy of judgment. Besides, Lord Incarnadine would
have wanted it that way."

Murmurs of "Hear, hear!" around the table.

"Well-spoken, Lord Morrel," Trent said. "Then how do
you propose to deal with the situation? What happens until
a regent is appointed? And what happens then?"

A man across from Tragg rose. "Your Highness. I think
we are all in unspoken agreement as to the best course of
action."

"Go on, Lord Baldon. What's the best course of action?"

"The Council as a whole, making up a Board of King's
Regents, will govern until such time as a suitable regent is
found. There is historical precedent for this. Twelve hundred years ago the untimely death of Ervoldt VII left the
infant Arven his successor. The King's Council appointed
various regents over the next twenty years—"

"Yes," Trent broke in, "as a dozen factions battled for control. There was one damned palace coup after another."

"Until Arven came of age; then—"

"Baldon, don't you think it would be a good idea to avoid that kind of hugger-mugger?"

"Of course, Highness," Lord Baldon agreed hastily. "Of course! But—" He cast his eyes around the table. "I see nothing but civilized men here. After all, these are modern times. We are not barbarians. We are not brigands. This is a democratic age."

Trent said, "But this isn't a democracy, nor should it be. The Lord of Perilous holds ultimate power. The castle is the source of all magic. One man must hold stewardship over that power. It cannot be shared. The saw about too many cooks also applies to magicians, Baldon."

"There is something to that," said the extremely old and wizened man to Trent's immediate right.

Trent turned to him. "Thank you, Lord Yorvil."

Yorvil smiled toothlessly. "Oh, I still have a thing or two to say, even at my age, that is not completely the product of an addled brain."

"Your contributions are always welcome, I assure you. How old are you, by the way?"

"I am in my seven hundred and sixth year, Highness."

Trent was surprised. "I had no idea. Are you quite sure you're not immortal?"

"I am happy to say that I will die this winter. The soothsayers have foretold it."

"Oh. I'm . . ."

"Fret not, good my lord. *'Glad did I live and gladly die, and I laid me down with a will.'* "*

Trent laughed. "Yorvil, you'll probably dance on my grave."

*From a poem by Robert Louis Stevenson.

Eyes twinkling, Yorvil replied, "If so, it will be a pavane, my lord prince."

"On the contrary. I think you can still do a fine gavotte."

Yorvil chortled merrily.

The smile left Trent's face as he leaned forward, elbows on the buffed tabletop.

"Back to business. My lords, I find your plan, if you can call it that, unacceptable. The last thing this castle needs is to be thrown into a dither, a prolonged period of uncertainty fraught with internecine squabbling and general palace intrigue. That's nonsense of the first water. I won't have it."

"But, Your Highness . . ."

"Tragg, are you going to tell me that I'm not the heir apparent and don't have a leg to stand on? That I ought to mind my own business and get back to my trade—?"

"Oh, never, Your Highness," Tragg protested. "Never!"

Trent sat back and chuckled. "Imagine, a prince of the realm going into trade. How positively déclassé. I guess that renders me beneath contempt. And I won't even mention my marrying a commoner!" He scanned the room once again, sizing it up. "Nevertheless . . ." He drifted off momentarily, then brought his attention around again. "Nevertheless, this hotel clerk is giving you an ultimatum."

All heads turned.

"Ultimatum?" Baldon said, gray brows raised almost to indignant heights.

"I might as well lay all my cards on the table. I want to rule. Hell, I've always wanted to. And now here's my chance. I want the regency, on my terms. Or . . ."

"Or?" Tragg said quietly.

Trent's eyes had narrowed. There was a hint of menace in them. Now they widened and a slow smile spread across his face. He sat back, lifted his left foot and rested it on the edge of the table.

"Or I'll press my claims to the throne again. Legally, this time. Through the courts."

Dismayed grumblings around the table.

Trent's grin was sly. "Oh, you don't like that, do you? Yes, years of litigation, the courts in an uproar. The expense. The uncertainty. Poor magistrates gnashing teeth in their sleep. The *expense*."

Morrel mopped the translucent skin of his forehead. "The barristers' fees will eat us alive!"

"Oh yes, oh yes." Trent's manner was airy and casual.

"Your Highness," Baldon pleaded. "I beg of you, spare us this travail. This was all settled *years* ago!"

"Not by my lights. Nothing was settled except that Incarnadine was crowned and I wasn't. I didn't get so much as an invite to the coronation. Pity, I would have RSVPed and everything. Had an outfit all picked out."

It was Tragg's turn to plead. "My lord prince, we cannot have this."

"Then make me Prince Regent, and I'll lay off. It's easy."

Yorvil cackled appreciatively. Trent grinned at him.

Baldon turned to the man on his left. "Lord Hivelt, as Royal Counsel and Barrister General, how do you assess the legal merits of His Highness's claim?"

Hivelt's long hair was salt-and-pepper, though he looked not much younger than the rest of the ministers. His voice, however, was strong and resonant. "It's hard to say, my Lord. There is the fraternal twin question to be considered."

Tragg huffed. "That old chestnut! A legal chimera."

"I'm not so sure," Hivelt said.

Baldon asked, "But how would you rate His Highness's chances for making good his claim to the throne?"

Hivelt shook his head. "Ah, that's impossible to say. He does have a prima facie case, after all—"

"Really, Hivelt!" Tragg's eyes were sharply admonitory.

Hivelt shrugged. "It's the truth. As His Highness said, it would be a long bout of litigation, probably dragging on for years. There's no telling which way it would come out. Eventually, he might very well succeed in wresting the throne from Prince Brandon."

Expressions of chagrin were exchanged around the table.

Baldon leaned forward. "Your Highness, you spoke of terms?"

Trent answered, "Yes. Conditions under which I will take the job. The term of regency will extend beyond Brandon's attainment of majority. In other words, he won't be crowned until . . ."

Trent broke off and laughed again.

"Yes, Highness," Tragg urged. "Until . . . ?"

"Well, until I either croak or get tired of the whole mess and abdicate . . . uh, step down. Then Brandon becomes Lord of Perilous and king of the realms therein."

Outrageous was the word most whispered around the table.

"Oh, come, gentle lords," Trent said. "I know it's a grab for power. I admit it. It's a scam, a ruse. I'll be king in all but name, not just regent. But I've been waiting for just such an opportunity all my life. Now it's here, knocking away, and I'm making my move. All legal and proper. I think I deserve the throne, and I think I was wronged by having the throne denied me. It's that simple. You may detest my methods, but my motives are pure. I simply want what is rightfully mine, what was granted me by the divine grace of the gods."

" 'Legal and proper,' " Tragg scoffed. "There is a term for what you are about."

"Oh, I'm not afraid of the word. One man's blackmail is another's friendly persuasion. Sure, I'm railroading you.

But you guys . . . pardon my lapsing into cant. You're all past masters at the art of strong-arming. You wouldn't be in the positions you're in if you weren't. Why this sudden pretense of being shocked when the wrestling match starts going against you?"

"With respect, I object to your choice of metaphor."

Trent took his foot from the table. "Forget the rhetorical devices. I'm making you an offer you shouldn't refuse. I'll settle for a souped-up regency in exchange for signing papers to the effect that I relinquish all claims to the Siege Perilous, in perpetuity, in aeternum, et cetera. Do we have a deal?"

At the end of his patience, Tragg protested, "His Highness wants both sides of his bread buttered. He wants us to choose between making him king de facto and entertaining his pretensions to kingship de jure. In short, make him king now or wait till he outmaneuvers us and steals the throne later. Sir, we are damned if we do or don't!"

"Damned right. That's it in the proverbial nutshell. I have you guys over a barrel and you know it."

Yorvil cackled fiendishly, slapping the table.

Trent looked at him, amused.

Hivelt surveyed the room, tallying silent assent. "My lords, shall we all say that we'll take it into consideration?"

Tragg's fist hit the table. "I'll not stand for it!"

Hivelt sighed. "One objection, then. Any others?"

"I want an answer soon," Trent said.

"Surely, sir, you'll let us consult in private before—"

"Of course, of course." Trent's smile suddenly left him. "About the coroner's inquest . . ."

"There will be no autopsy," Hivelt said.

"Huh? Why?"

"Canon law. No mutilation of the king's body is permitted."

"Not even when there's some question as to the cause of death?"

"No. Under no circumstances."

"What does Dr. Mirabilis think the cause of death was?"

"He will make a preliminary post mortem report in a few hours. However, he's limited in what he can do."

"Has he said *anything*? Guesses?"

"He did say something about heart failure."

Trent snorted. "That's a big help."

"We'll know eventually," Hivelt said, shrugging. "Mirabilis says he has plenty of non-intrusive procedures."

"Well, that's something."

"His Highness's solicitude concerning his brother is most touching," Tragg said. The irony fairly oozed.

Trent's manner had undergone a rapid change. He looked uneasy. But he managed a crooked grin. "Tragg, that was right over the plate. Not your usual breaking ball. Why don't you come right out and say I had him murdered?"

"Again, His Highness's choice of metaphor eludes me." Tragg sniffed.

Baldon intervened, "I'm sure Lord Tragg means no such imputation."

"I know he does. But no matter. My lords, I must leave. Uh, one thing more. The funeral."

"A grand state funeral, of course, Highness."

Trent nodded. "Yeah, with all the trimmings, I expect. When?"

"According to canon law, the body must lie in state for ten days—"

"Ten days? Preposterous. And I'll bet no embalming is allowed either."

"Correct, Highness. But a spell of preservation will be cast."

"Right," Trent answered dubiously. "Still, ten days . . ."

Baldon raised his hands in helpless appeal. "There is no relief from canon law. Am I not right, Renalto?"

The small man next to Baldon nodded. "As Minister Plenipotentiary for Religious Affairs, it is my duty to see that canon law is obeyed to the letter. I shall do so."

"Very well," Trent said. "I'll not object to any of the mummery if I get a quick reply to my proposal."

Hivelt said, "I think we have a deal on that, at least. We . . . Your Royal Highness, is anything wrong?"

A rivulet of sweat was making its way down the line of Trent's jaw. He gave his head a brisk shake. "Not a thing. I have to go. Messenger your decision to me as soon as possible."

"You will be where, sir?"

"Club Sheila. I must leave the castle for a while, but I'll be back."

Trent got up and strode out of the room. The door slammed shut behind him.

Baldon said, "The curse. He can't stay in the castle for long."

"And he wants to be king!" Tragg looked around. "Will no one back me?"

"Back you in what?" Hivelt said.

"In thwarting the bastard, of course!"

Lord Renalto put his fingers to his lips. "Tragg, curb your tongue!"

"I care not whose spies are eavesdropping. The man must be stopped."

"How?" Hivelt asked.

"By whatever means at our disposal!"

Hivelt groaned, shaking his head. "I share Trent's aversion to squabbling and intrigue. I'm inclined to cave in to him just to avoid all that."

"Then you are a coward, sir!"

Hivelt smiled weakly. "A seasoned one. I have spent three hundred years perfecting my talents."

Baldon said dolefully, "The legal fees will be ruinous."

"A pox on the legal fees!" Tragg shouted.

"If we challenge Trent's claim, the fees will be extracted from our personal salaries," Baldon said grimly. "And if we don't challenge, Trent will be king, not just regent."

Hivelt said, "It seems, my lords, that we are between the rocks and the whirlpool. I vote for the rocks. I say we go for Trent's deal. Last time: Are there any other objections?"

"I am in debt to my ears already," Baldon muttered. He had commiseration around the table.

Tragg looked left, then right. He banged the table, rose, and stalked out of the room. The door slammed again.

Everyone leaned back and exhaled. There was a sense of relief, however dour the upshot.

"Somebody yank the bell pull, please?" Hivelt said.

"Let's wait till after lunch," Morrel suggested. "We have that much face to save, at least. Make him sweat a little longer."

"Very well," Hivelt said, rising. "I eat a lot when I get depressed. When I eat a lot, I eat Oriental. How about you guys?"

"That suits me," Morrel said brightly.

The sundry ministers of the King's Privy Council began to file out of the room.

When the door closed again, only Lord Yorvil was left.

He was still cackling to himself, smiling craftily, drumming the table with one wrinkled, skeletal hand.

Spot Quiz No. 1

Fill in the blanks:

1. The setting of the story is Castle _____.
2. The master of this strange, enchanted castle is Lord _____.
3. The magical doorways in the castle, leading to other worlds, are called _____.
4. The opening scene in this story takes place in the _____ Hall.
5. In the opening chapter, four characters are playing bridge. They are _____, _____, _____, and _____.
6. In the game of contract bridge, partners sometimes signal the strength or weakness of their hands by means of bidding conventions. One of these is known as the _____ convention.
7. In contract bridge, a contract in which no suit is specified is known as a _____ contract.
8. Lord Peter Thaxton, a minor character in this story, was elevated to the peerage (got his title) because he

was instrumental in solving the _____ Castle murders.

9. Jousting tournaments are usually fought with a long, spearlike medieval weapon known as a _____.

10. Adults who read fantasy novels are thought by some psychologists to be in a phase of arrested adolescent _____.

True or False?

1. The characters in this book are lifelike and convincing. ____

2. Gene likes action and adventure. ____

3. Snowclaw is a very good bridge player for a nonhuman. ____

4. Flinging-toads are specially bred for competition. ____

5. Castle Perilous has exactly 143,999 magical doorways. ____

6. The average commercial tuna boat is 40 feet from stem to stern. ____

7. The chief export of Tierra del Fuego is hemp. ____

8. Linda is an adept sorceress. ____

9. Osmirik is a bit on the anal-retentive side. ____

10. The price of this book is outrageous for a cheesy paperback. ____

Essay Questions (Keep your answer under 500 words.)

1. Discuss some of the methods the author employs to make a totally fantastic tale believable. Does he suc-

ceed? If not, where does he go wrong? Relate all of this to what Aristotle says about verisimilitude in his *Poetics*.

2. The chapters featuring the person walking across the featureless plane—what is all that about? Is it fair for an author to be so vague and sketchy and keep the reader in suspense? Discuss ways of dealing with this problem.

3. Discuss the possible meaning of the epigraph of this book. (The epigraph is the poem-fragment quoted just before the text of the book begins.) Relate it to the story, then comment on how well-read and erudite the author must be.

For Group Discussion

1. Explore the possible animal-rights issues involved in the concept of a "toad-fling."

2. Is bridge an elitist game?

3. Have significant contributions to Western culture been made by non-Italians?

MINE

THE DOOR HISSED shut behind them.

When he saw it begin to close, Gene began a desperate lunge to catch it, then stopped short. Before he took two strides the darkness had closed in.

"Great," he said. "Right out of a B movie."

"A what?"

Before he could get his penlight out of its pouch in his utility belt, a pale halo of luminescence relieved the gloom. The source, he was interested to learn, turned out to be two luminous strips on the front of his companion's blue-and-silver pressure suit. They emitted a strange greenish glow, cold and faint, but provided enough light to illuminate the surroundings: a large wedge-shaped chamber with lots of empty racks and shelves. A second door was set into the inside wall.

"Handy gadgets, those," he commented.

"Standard," she said. "Are you going to keep claiming that it was magic that got us in here?"

"Not if it annoys you."

"Not at all. It's just not a very convincing cover story for the obviously advanced circuit-scanning implant you have. It is a bionic chip, isn't it?"

"If you insist. Now where can we find that security system?"

"Use your implant to trace it to the master computer."

"Yeah."

She looked around. "No alarms are going off, and I find that rather strange."

"Well, the facilitation spell is still working. Actually, I supplied the lock with the correct security code, so the system probably thinks that we have a right to be here."

"Then we'd better stop talking about it. The system is intelligent enough to learn from our conversation that it was fooled."

"As I said, the spell's still working, and will continue to do so for a bit longer. It'll smooth our way, make things happen in our favor. But it'll wear off eventually. So, let's get busy."

"When it wears off, can't you simply cast another spell?"

"Yeah, but it won't be as effective. Magic loses potency with overuse, you know."

"Well, no, I didn't know that. Interesting."

He chuckled. "You're more than a little skeptical."

"Not as much as you think. Is 'magic' your word for psychic ability?"

"Hmm. Well, there is some mental discipline involved, but 'psychic' is the wrong word for me. It's a supermarket tabloid buzzword. . . . Uh, never mind. Call it whatever you want. What it is, is magic, pure and simple. The real stuff. Let's see what's behind this other door."

The inner door was not locked but had a complicated levered latch. Gene worked the mechanism and pulled the door open. It led into an oblong room with rack after empty rack that might once have held electronic instruments. He walked between the rows and came out, then stood looking at the bare counters that ran along the walls.

He said, "Scavengers?"

"Possibly, but it looks too clean. The stuff was probably stripped when the installation was closed."

"Was this communications, do you think?"

"No," she said. "Maybe a laboratory for mineral analysis. There is an outside chance they left the communications gear. The place hasn't been left open to the elements. There might be plans to restart operations or convert the place into something else."

"They were pretty thorough in stripping the place."

"A multiphone is a huge piece of equipment. Sometimes it's more trouble than it's worth to tear one out. Let's look for the communications shack."

There were other rooms on the first floor, all offering little but empty packing crates and other debris. They found an elevator but passed it up in favor of spiral stairs, which they mounted warily, Gene leading the way with his flashlight. The second floor was apportioned between more laboratory space and a number of cubicles: offices or sleeping quarters; it was hard to tell which until they arrived on the third floor, where, in rooms even more cozy, some metal cots sans mattresses remained. There were more rooms off to the right, and they walked on into the darkness. It was a big building.

"Here it is," she said, stepping through a doorway.

Most of this room was like the rest—denuded racks and shelves—the only difference being a large array of cylinders and spheres running along the left wall.

"That's a multiphone?" Gene asked.

"The resonating chamber and radiation sources, at least," she said. "And the control circuits"—she knelt before a metal cabinet and ran a finger along a vertical opening that once might have housed an electronics module—"are gone."

She sighed and settled cross-legged into a sitting position. She hung her head and closed her eyes.

Gene played the flashlight's beam around the room. A few stray nuts and bolts, one or two funny-looking vacuum tubes, if that's what they were (he doubted it), an empty plastic box, a length of plastic tape, dust, grit . . .

He looked at her. She sat unmoving.

He listened. Nothing. No enemies approaching. This seemed a safe place. He wondered about the security system. The spell hadn't worn off yet. He wondered what would happen when it did.

"What do you want to do?" he asked her.

She was silent, motionless.

"I don't even know your name," he said.

She had no comment.

"Uh, then again, maybe you don't want me to know your name."

She opened her eyes and looked up at him. "Who and what are you?"

"I'm Gene Ferraro. What am I? Just a . . . wanderer. A drifter. And you?"

"Sativa."

"Nice name. That the only name?"

She looked down again. Her voice sounded tired as she said, "Scions of aristocratic houses don't have surnames, properly speaking, but I'm of the House of Hemlin. It's a big, important family, with many members prominent in Dominion politics." Her tone seemed to imply that this wasn't very remarkable or at all important.

"Is it all right if I think of you as Sativa Hemlin?"

"Feel free."

"Almost sounds like an Earth name."

"Earth?"

"Where I'm from."

"Oh. Never heard of it. Sorry."

"No reason you should have. Mind telling me why you're so important to the Irregulars? —Oh, God, wait a minute."

She looked up again. "What?"

"Uh, you're not going to tell me you have the secret plans to the Death Star, are you?"

"The what?"

He shook his head vigorously, dismissing the whole notion. "Nothing, nothing."

"I don't have any secrets of any sort."

"For a second there, I was a little worried. Thought I'd walked into some weird aspect."

"You're making no sense whatsoever."

"Forget it. Private joke, just kidding."

Gene paced once in a circle, idly sweeping the beam around the room.

"You're a very strange person," Sativa said, "but I suppose I owe you my life. For what that's worth."

"Don't sweat it. You still haven't told me why they're after you."

"I'd make a perfect hostage. I hold a hereditary seat in the Upper Chamber of the Dominion legislature. I also hold the permanent rank of Wing Leader in the Dominion Near-Space Guards. Last but not least, I'm the daughter of the Outworld Proconsul. My mother is the highest Dominion official governing the hundreds of worlds not directly connected to the Thread."

"So you're one choice VIP. Very Important Package. What's the Thread?"

Sativa lifted unbelieving eyes. "You must be joking."

"I think I told you that I'm from a world that is very far away."

"How far? Could your world be off the Thread completely? If so, how did you get here? This is not an inhabited planet."

"I got here . . . basically through a spacetime anomaly which was brought about by the same powers that fooled the security lock."

"Magic again?"

"Yes, magic. It's the truth, even though you don't buy it, not for the briefest moment."

"I did, for the briefest moment," she said, "when you mumbled that nonsense. I suppose that was an incantation."

"Yeah, sort of. Well, yes, that's exactly what it was. It serves only to focus the mind. Come to think of it, magic is a mostly mental discipline. It very well could be psychic, much as I loathe that word."

"Whatever." She sighed. "Very well. Even though, frankly, I think you're lying, I'll tell you what the Thread is. It is a fracture in the fabric of spacetime . . . I *know* you know what *that* is, so don't feign ignorance, please. A crack, a fault, if you will. Better to say, a seam in the continuum. It is one of an unknown number of such. These seams were formed—so the astrophysicists tell us—in the early stages of the formation of the universe itself. They were produced when the primordial flux of matter—or energy, I should say—went through rapid changes from one state to another. Since the efforts could not propagate instantaneously, sections of the flux changed independently of others. Seams, or faults, appeared between the sections. Like the surface of a pond freezing. It doesn't all freeze at the same time. It forms plates. Think of a multidimensional equivalent to that process. The plates of spacetime are bounded by threads."

"Cosmic strings."

"Yes? That's what you call them?"

"Just a theory where I come from. Now I understand. Okay. And the Thread is used for interstellar travel, faster than light?"

"You grasp things quickly for one who prides himself on ignorance. Yes, the regions of space near the Thread are anomalous, and, with the proper technology, can be exploited for space travel."

"How?"

"Basically you pilot your ship near enough to the inner singularity of the Thread so that the extreme gravitational force pulls the ship along. The intense distortions of spacetime in those regions produce strange effects, most of which are not completely understood. One of the effects is superluminal travel. But if you get too close to the singularity, you die. Understand?"

"I think so. Nifty."

Sativa frowned at this word, then shrugged. "The Dominion of Worlds is sometimes called the Beads Along the Thread. The Thread runs through several galaxies—"

"Travel between galaxies? Now there's a radical concept. You're talking about huge distances, aren't you?"

She nodded. "But they are nothing to the Thread. The Thread obliterates space—and time."

"I like it, I like it. Now, obviously there's a war going on."

"Good observation," she said.

"A rebellion."

"Of a sort."

"And the Irregulars are the rebels."

"They're criminals."

"Well, you're part of the establishment under siege. You would tend to feel that way about them."

"It isn't a feeling. They are a pack of cutthroats posing as noble freedom fighters. They have duped everyone who has lent them support."

"Do they have support?"

"Enormous support. They have their supporters in the legislature itself, some of them in the Upper Chamber."

"Interesting."

"Their cause is widely held to be just. I, personally, think they have already won. The Dominion is doomed. It's only a matter of time. But some of us fight on."

"To save the Dominion."

"Yes. Some are still foolish enough to believe in it and in the principles for which is stands."

"Which are?"

"You want a lecture on government?"

"Not if you don't want to lecture me," he said, "though maybe we should talk about more important matters. Like, what do we do now?"

Sativa lifted her shoulders. "I suppose you turn me in for whatever you can bargain out of the Irregulars."

"Forget that noise. Do we hide in the mine or take to the hills?"

She shrugged again. "It matters little. They will find us no matter what."

"Then our best bet is the mine," he said.

"Is it? I suppose. It will simply delay my capture. There is only one way out, really. Please give me my gun."

"Forget about shooting yourself. I won't let them take you."

She looked up at him. "No? Strange." She made motions to get up.

"Rest a minute," he said, settling down beside her.

She gave him a long, questioning look. "Why are you helping me?"

He leaned over and kissed her full lips.

"Sorry," he said. "I don't know why I did that. Well, yes, I do know. You're tremendously attractive."

"You want me? Then take me. I have no means to resist you."

"I'd hardly want you under those circumstances."

"If that is the reason you're helping me, fine. At least I can understand that."

"I don't usually take advantage of women."

"You like men?"

"Not what I meant."

"Then take me." She grabbed his hand and pressed it to her crotch.

The material of the suit she wore was thinner then he'd expected it to be.

"You know how to get right to the point," he said.

"We don't have very much time."

"Your wound," he said, running his hand along the bloody tear.

"It will be all right."

She touched a few spots on the front of the suit and the whole thing opened up with a ripping sound like Velcro. He didn't see any Velcro. She was naked underneath.

His hand went immediately to the laceration along her side. It was long and ugly, but had just missed doing any real damage. The bleeding had stopped, and the wound was already scabbing over. Then his hand went to her small breasts.

"Yes, take me now, before they rape me."

"I won't let them. You're beautiful, do you know?"

"Some say."

"Do you have a husband?"

"Yes. He is an artist."

"I don't do married women. This is ridiculous."

"What is ridiculous about it?"

"Nothing. Sorry. I didn't mean that you're—"

"Then make love to me."

"Yes, I will."

UNDERWORLD

HE WAITED, but did not know for what.

He waited on the banks of a wide river. Above, darkness, with a suggestion of limit, as of a roof. This place might be a vast cavern. Huge rocks lined the river bank, save on the narrow gravel strand where he stood watching the outer darkness for signs of life.

He did not think there was much life here.

The waters of the river were black, gray-black near the river bank, shading to inky-black farther out. The current was slow. Shallow wavelets angled into shore from his right, lapping the gravel with a sound like a dog at its water bowl. The river flowed silently, inexorably. Darkness and silence.

He wondered how he could make anything out at all. There was no source of light. This, he decided, was the realm of darkness visible.

What a striking turn of phrase, he thought.

He also wondered why he sensed a roof to the place. Perhaps it was simply a dark sky. But no; this place was underground. Deep underground. There was a hushed stillness, a quietude that could not be explained otherwise.

He listened to the water suckling at the river bank, feeding on its substance. He stamped the ground. The place on which he stood was real enough. He wasn't dreaming. He decided to defer trying to answer the question of how he had come to this place. Nor would he have a go at some corollary puzzles: Where was this place? What he he been doing before this?

Who was he?

Who?

No, better to put all that off indefinitely. One could not properly ask questions with so few facts at one's disposal. It was better to wait, to observe, to gather information. Only then would it be possible to formulate a hypothesis.

No, don't ask: *Wait for what? Observe what?* Although there was nothing here but the perceivable absence of light, he was sure something would turn up. Something would appear out of obscurity, and that something would be meaningful.

He looked out across the waters.

Nothing.

He sought out something to sit on and found a suitably flat rock at the edge of the strand. He eased himself down and listened to the water. It said nothing to him. Silence closed in, and he thought he could hear the beating of his heart. This mildly surprised him, because he had somehow got the notion that he had no heart. He considered the matter again and decided that what he heard might have been something else, some deep underground pulse. The throb of machinery. That notion struck him as unlikely. He listened again. Yes, it seemed to be his own heart. Puzzled as to why he had failed to think of it before, he put his left index finger against his right wrist. A pulse! He was alive. His body was real.

But why wouldn't it be real? No answer to that.

This place struck a chord in him. Something about it stirred him deep inside; yet it smacked of the unreal. This was all supposed to mean something. He knew not what.

Resolving to find out what it all meant, he cast himself deep into thought.

There was something out in the darkness.

First, merely a suggestion, a black shape on black. Then, movement, difficult to detect but growing ever perceptible. Slow, steady movement, like that of a boat on water.

It was a boat. The form took shape out of the shadows. It was a long, narrow boat, an elongated skiff, its sharp prow parting the dark waters. A single figure stood at the stern. Gradually, the figure's man-shape revealed itself; but the outline was something more than an ordinary man's. It towered a head and a half taller than workaday mortals, and the arms that grasped the tiller-oar (for the huge wooden beam seemed to be both) were sculpted of magnificent sinews.

The boat could hold a number of passengers; perhaps as many as seven or eight. Ten with crowding and the risk of capsizing.

The figure at the tiller now grew to superhuman proportions, not so much in size as in fearful aspect. The gray-bearded face grew discernible. There was not much humanity in that face. It looked like a mask. Yet it was somehow lifelike. An animated mask. The eyes seemed to glow. In them was the gleam of intelligence but not much else. No pity; surely no compassion. However, neither was there malevolence.*

This was a businessman.

*The extreme tip of Latin America is an endlessly fascinating area of the world.

The boat approached the shore at a sharp angle, heading in toward the left edge of the strand.

He got up and walked to the edge of the strand and there discovered that a stone jetty extended a short distance out from the river bank. It could be a natural formation, he decided, though he was not at all sure. The boatman swung the tiller around and the long craft aligned its length with the edge of the jetty.

He walked out from shore over water-smoothed boulders.

"Greetings," he said when he reached the boat.

The boatman nodded his great head. His hair was an unruly mass of gray.

"What's across the river?"

The boatman heaved his huge shoulders. "I know not, nor care." The voice was resonantly deep.

"Is it your job to take people across?"

A nod. "That it is."

"Then, I suppose . . ."

The boatman's left arm made a sweeping invitation.

"Come aboard my boat. But first—"

"Yes?"

"You must pay."

"Ah, yes. Of course."

For the first time he realized that he was naked.

"I'm afraid I have no money."

The boatman's dark brow lowered. "Then you may not cross."

"Pity. May I ask how payment is usually made?"

"They take from their eyes coins, like golden tears."

"I see." He reached and touched his eyes. "I have none."

"Then you may not cross."

"This appears hopeless. What can one offer in lieu of coins?"

The boatman's voice was flat. "Nothing."

"You're quite sure? Is there no service I can perform? No favor that I might bestow?"

"None."

"Have you no needs?"

"Not many. Those which I have are met with money."

"Why was I brought here?"

The boatman shook his head in response. "I know not."

"It seems as though I should cross, that I was meant to cross."

"So it would seem," the boatman agreed.

"Yet I am barred from this possibility."

"Again, so it would seem."

"And you have no explanation?"

"None."

He regarded the boatman for a moment. The boatman's cold gaze met his. At length the huge man turned and grasped the tiller. Angling it toward the rocks, he began to push the boat out into the river.

"Wait."

The boatman turned from his task. "Why?"

"There must be something I can do for you. You say your needs are met with money. Have you no other requirements, no yearnings, such that cannot be satisfied with material gain?"

"Such as?"

"Companionship?"

The boatman grunted.

He persisted: "You are never lonely?"

"Never."

"Is this all you do? Plying the river, taking souls to and fro?"

"Yes. Why do you ask?"

"You never grow weary?"

"Never."

"You are never bored?"

The boatman was silent, his cold gaze deflecting.

"What say you to that?"

The boatman looked up. "The task does at times grow tedious."

"Ah. Then I can help."

The boatman looked dubious. "How so?"

"I can entertain you."

The boatman again gave a skeptical grunt.

"I can tell you stories."

"Stories?"

"Yes. I know many."

"Stories of what, and of what interest would they be to me?"

"You won't know until I tell you. Stories of other realms, other regions. Other worlds than this. You, who know only those dark, despairing waters, would naturally be interested."*

"This I doubt," the boatman said.

"I guarantee that you would find it diverting."

The boatman considered the matter. Then he said, "Tell me of these things."

"Take me across."

"First tell me some of these stories of other worlds."

"I will not. I will begin only if you let me onto the boat."

The boatman thought long on it. At last he said, "Get in."

He ambled down from the rocks and boarded. Choosing a seat amidships, he sat and watched as the boatman pushed the craft out into the slow, shadowy waters of the river.

---

*To my knowledge, the author has never done a book on Tierra del Fuego.

When the river bank had receded into the darkness, the boatman said, "Now. I crave a bit of diversion. Tell me a story."

He drew a breath and began.

"A guy walks into a bar with a duck under his arm . . ."

CRYPT

SOMETHING SPLIT THE darkness. A vertical line of light, widening.

The door of the dark chamber creaked open and a figure stood in the door frame, outlined against the light in the corridor outside. It was a man in a plumed hat, who then entered, stopping midway between the door and a half-illuminated table.

A flame appeared, limning a face, an upraised arm sleeved in green silk, and a hand holding a butane cigarette lighter.

The man in green approached the table, on which stood a candelabra holding five half-burnt tapers. He lit one taper, then another. A third. The room brightened.

He clicked the butane light off and slipped it into a pocket, then turned about to take in the surroundings. Shelves of books abounded in the chamber. Other shelving held a gallimaufry of knickknacks and oddments, games and gadgets, curios and other quaint conversation pieces. Maps, charts, drawings, and paintings, interspersed with a few photographs of scantily clad women, covered the stone walls.

It was a pleasantly cluttered room, but there was about it a feeling of disuse. The air was still, musty and cryptlike.

He crossed and closed the door. Taking off his cape, he hung it on a clothes tree to the right of the door. The hat he parked on a large mirrored hatrack tacked to the wall, where it found several colleagues to keep it company.

Narrowing his eyes, he scanned the room, as if trying to sense something invisible. He angled his head slightly, listening not so much to outside sounds as to his own inner voices.

"No," he said finally. "Not even Inky."

Satisfied, he crossed the room slowly, noting familiar objects not seen in quite a while. Lingering to look at a framed photograph of an attractive young woman, he smiled faintly, fondly.

"Long ago and far away."

He paused in the middle of the room and made a sweeping motion with his right hand.

"Rise and shine, everyone."

Oddly enough, the room suddenly took on a more comfortable aspect. Perhaps it had brightened a bit. Perhaps not.

He touched a framed astronomical chart on the far wall and swung it open like a door. Recessed in the wall behind it was a conventional-looking circular safe door, complete with handle and combination lock.*

He rubbed his fingers against his lapels, blew on them. Gingerly, he reached to lay sensitized fingertips on the combination spinner. But stopped just short.

---

*Tierra del Fuego is not a nation. It is a group of islands owned partly by Argentina and Chile. The struggle for Tierra del Fuegan independence, however, goes on.

"Open up in there."

The door popped open. He reached in, withdrew some papers wrapped in string. He went to a nearby writing desk and examined these documents briefly. Leaving them on the desk, he returned to the safe.

"Anyone been fooling around in here?"

"Not a soul, boss," a small, comical voice came from the darkness inside the hole.

"Any supernatural intrusions?"

"Nope."

"Sure?"

"Sure, boss. Hey . . . boss?"

He halted a motion to shut the door. "What?"

"When can I get sprung from this place?"

"Getting restless?"

"Kind of."

"Trouble is, I still need this safe safeguarded, so to speak. How long's it been?"

"Oh, going on a hundred fifty years, boss."

"That all? You're immortal, I'm not. When I shuffle off, you're free."

"Don't want to bring up an indelicate issue, boss, but how much longer you figure to be around?"

"You selling insurance?"

"Ballpark figure."

"Five hundred seems to be the upper limit in my family. Short-lived."

"Oh. Okay, thanks."

"By your reckoning, you'll be out in no time. Keep a stiff . . . well, whatever."

"Whatever."

He closed the safe door and gave the tumblers a spin.

"Man, I need a drink."

The liquor cabinet in a near corner took the cue immediately. Hands—disembodied hands, it was to be hoped (the alternative being an altogether disconcerting possibility)—extruded from several cavities, busying themselves with bottles and glasses. A cork popped, liquid gurgled.

He went to the cabinet, took the glass of amber fluid and downed it in a gulp.

"Another, please."

Another was poured.

When finished he let out a rasping breath and set the emptied glass down.

A table set into a nook drew his attention now. Heaped on the table was a jumble of antiquated electronic components juxtaposed with gold candelabra and brass incense burners. He lit the candles, then fetched incense from a nearby shelf and charged the burners.

Soon the nook was aglow with candlelight and fragrant with exotic odors.

He took a seat and flipped a switch on one of the components. Somewhere within the thicket of tubes and wiring, a tinny speaker crackled and hissed.

He bent his head toward an upright microphone.

"This is Trent, calling Dad. Come in, Dad."

The speaker emitted little but static.

He repeated the invocation.

The speaker popped and crackled.

"Calling Cawdor,* former King of the Realms Perilous. This is Trent, your eldest son. I wish to speak with you."

He reiterated several times before the speaker gave forth.

. . . *Trent? Is th*—?

"Dad! Dad, come in! This is Trent. Can you hear me?"

---

*Cawdor is the name of the castle in Shakespeare's *Macbeth*. Castles seem to be one of the author's abiding crotchets. (Satellite photos have shown that there are no castles in Tierra del Fuego.)

. . . —ell are you calling on? . . . just barely make you . . .

"Dad, I want to talk with you. Can you grant me a visitation?"

. . . Say again?

"I want to talk with you. Can you grant me a visitation?"

The response was garbled.

"Please, Dad. I'm in a spot."

So spit it out.

"Not in the clear. Not over the ether, especially on this contraption."

Again, the answer was mostly unintelligible.

"Dad?"

Not much but sputtering in reply.

"Shit. Come in. Come in, Cawdor, King of the—"

Trent smacked the table. He fiddled with a knob or two.

"Damn it all to hell."

He sat back and ruminated for a moment.

Trent, dearest.

Trent spun around.

"Mom!"

You should have called me first, dear. You and your father still aren't on speaking terms, at least as far as Cawdor is concerned.

Trent snapped off the receiver. He rose and approached the table where the shade of his mother sat.

She was as beautiful as she had been in life: light brown hair, oval face, blue eyes, thin straight nose. Her features were blurred a bit, however; the effect was not unlike a photograph taken with a refraction filter. It was as if she were somewhere else, and this a mere transmitted simulacrum. And in fact this was so.

Trent walked off to pour himself another drink, then

approached the table again. Passing the hearth, he waved a hand; flames sprang to life out of grayish logs.

He stopped short of the table. "I'm sorry. Can I offer you—?"

Nothing for me, dearest. Do sit down. That fire is nice and cheery.

"You're sure? Well, then."

Trent drew out a chair and sat. He sipped his whiskey.

His mother gave the room a glance. *What an interesting place you have here. I can't recall ever seeing it.*

"My sanctum sanctorum. Little hideout I outfitted when I was a kid. Used to come here to sulk, brood, and plot."

You used to do a lot of sulking and brooding. You were a moody child.

"So I was. I admit it."

I can see a lot of boyhood paraphernalia about. I think I recognize those ice skates. Didn't we—?

"You used to love to take me skating. We'd go to Zadar and skate the canals."

I remember. Yes, I loved to skate. I could cut a fancy figure as a girl.

"In more ways than one." He smiled.

She returned it. *Moody, but, as ever, charming.*

"Your Prince Charming, my princess."

Dearest Trent. You were my favorite. So handsome.

"Too bad Dad didn't feel the same way."

He loved you, too, Trent.

Trent sipped again before saying, "Pardon me if I emit a little derisory laughter."

He did. But I'm not going to spend the time necessary to change your mind on a matter that you made your mind up about a long time ago.

"Can't change my mind about a fact."

Be that as it may. She gave the room another glance. *Why are you here?*

"It's the only place in the castle where I can spend any amount of time."

Father's banishing spell?

"Yes. Here my local protective devices seem to offset it, for the most part. But I can't stay here for a prolonged period either. Consequently, I've been forced to spend most of the last hundred years or so outside the castle entirely."*

Where?

"Earth, a lot. Other places."

Where do you live now?

"An uncharted aspect."

How uncomfortable it must be for you. I hear you're married.

"Yes. An Earth woman. A commoner, as I'm certain you've heard."

I'm sure she's a nice girl.

"Women rather resent that appellation now."

Nice?

"No, 'girl.' "

They do? How old is she?

"Twenty-six."

Don't be silly.

"You think I'm robbing the cradle?"

That's not it, Trent. How old she is makes no difference as long as she's of marriageable age. It's just that there are problems associated with a mixed marriage.

Trent grinned crookedly. "Between ordinary mortals and demigods such as we, is that it?"

Don't be impious. We are powerful magicians, it's true,

---

*Despite all his references to exotic locales, the author has never been outside the continental United States (except for Canada, which counts as a foreign country, but not by much; unless you're talking about Quebec, which *is* a foreign country).

but hardly godlike. No, dear, I'm afraid our kind is all too venal and concupiscent.

"I agree. Compared to me, Sheila's a saint."

A nice name. As I said, I'm sure she's a wonderful girl for you—but, well, I hope you'll forgive my asking—was marriage absolutely necessary? I mean, a young man can be forgiven a few mistresses, after all—

"Mother, stifle it, please?"

Wherever did you pick up that vulgar cant? It sounds so coarse.

"I spent a long spell on Earth, among unsavory types. It rubs off."

We gave you the best education— She sighed. *Never mind, never mind. It is not for the dead to tell the living how to conduct their affairs.*

"Thank you."

But— She shrugged. *If that is so, why do you seek our counsel?*

"Frankly, for one reason. To get Dad to tell me how to lift the banishment spell. Inky died, as I'm sure you know—"

I didn't. Oh, dear.

"Eh?" Trent sat up sharply. "You don't know? But—"

Do you think omniscience is granted after death?

"Well, no, but . . ." Trent sat back. "Well, I assumed, wrongly it seems." Trent regarded his mother. "You don't look particularly upset."

The world must turn, death must come.

Trent grunted. "Silly of me to think you wouldn't have a different perspective on the issue."

I'm looking forward to seeing him.

"Yes, of course. But, as I was saying, I would be his son's regent, and I need the spell of banishment abrogated."

Oh, Trent. Not again.

"What again?"

This wanting-to-be-king business.

"Mother, please. I've every right to be."

Cawdor didn't think you had the temperament.

"I've the mettle, all right."

The mettle, yes. Prudence, forbearance, nice judgment, no.

"Nonsense."

Trent, I'm afraid nothing's changed.

"I've changed. Really. Even other people say so."

I'm sure you have. But at this late date— Trent, why do you want the Siege Perilous?

"It's rightfully mine. I'm the eldest son, and by rights I should have taken the throne."

You and Incarnadine were fraternal twins. He was born first.

Trent's fist thumped against the table. "That's not true!"

Dear, don't raise your voice.

"I'm sorry, Mother, but that's been a sore point with me for eons. *I* was born first, and I can prove it."

How?

Trent rose and went to the writing desk. He grabbed the sheaf of documents and returned.

"I have the attending physician's signed and sworn statement that I was the first out of the womb."

Oh, come, dear.

"Look at it! See?"

Yes, dear. I'm sure it's all in order.

"Dr. Philius. Recognize the name?"

Oh, I remember Dr. Philius well. I saw him, in fact, not too long ago.

"But he's years d— Oh, right. Well, you believe him, don't you?"

Well, of course, Trent. Dr. Philius would have no reason to lie.

"Well?"

He's simply mistaken. A mother knows. Inky was first.

"You were out like a light. How could you know?"

I realize you were there, too, Trent, but do you really doubt my word?

"Read it for yourself, right there. Dr. Philius says he gave you something to knock you out."

That he did, but it didn't work. He was much too reliant on pills and potions.

"Be that as it may, Philius was aware of the bearing this might have on the future succession, and he took pains to note who was born first. It was me, and he duly swears a statement to that effect and affixes his signature."

Nevertheless, Trent, dearest, Inky was first. I know. I saw his birthmark. A small, hourglass-shaped port-wine splotch on the left thigh. It was right in front of my nose when Philius laid him, all red and angry and yelling, across my chest. I thought it was the most beautiful little splotch I'd ever seen.

Trent was silent for a moment as he sat down. "Your memory is fogged. Philius wouldn't have made such a goof."

There's no doubt in my mind, Trent.

"If you'll forgive, Mother, I trust Philius's memory over yours."

Of course you do. This succession business has been an obsession with you since you were a lad. You see, I happen to have a very good memory.

"No doubt. You remember seeing a birthmark, all right, and it was Incarnadine's, but you don't remember when you saw it. Which was after I was born. I don't have a birthmark."

No, dear, it was before I delivered you. As I said, a mother knows these things. A mother remembers.

"You were exhausted and drugged to a stupor. It says here the labor was unusually difficult."

It was, Trent, but I told you—

He raised a hand. "Enough. Please. You said you didn't want to waste time tussling with me over a matter that I've quite made up my mind about, and I'm afraid this one fits that bill to a T."

She chuckled. *That I can see. We'll tussle no more.*

"All I ask is that you ask Dad to let me back into the castle."

Dear, your father is no longer part of this world, and neither am I. We inhabit quite a different realm, a cosmos greater than all the myriad worlds of the castle, vaster than all of Creation itself. You've no idea. The mundane doings on your plane of existence are of no concern to us. They are not within our proper sphere of concern. The living must be let alone to work out their own destinies. We cannot interfere.

"But it's Dad's doing that I can't live in the castle. Whatever wrong I did, surely I can be forgiven after so long a time."

Your father forgives you, Trent, for the trouble you caused. Though you may scoff at the notion, he loves you and has always loved you. That is not the issue.

"Then what the devil is the issue?"

Please don't use strong language with me.

"Apologies. Mother, really, I just don't understand."

She heaved her shoulders. *Yes, Trent, I know you don't. But you will, one day. You've a head on your shoulders and you'll eventually see that your father had nothing but your best interests at heart.*

"No doubt," Trent said dryly. He finished his whisky and set the glass back down. "Well."

Well, indeed. We've had a charming little sitdown, a nice little chat. But I must go.

"Goodbye, Mother."

Goodbye, Trent, darling. Trent, if it had been up to me, I would have ignored precedent and named you heir apparent. It means so much to you. But it wasn't up to me. A woman's lot—

"Yes, unluckily for me. All the more reason why I should boost women's rights."

Oh, it's not that women have no rights. In fact— Her hand rose to dismiss the matter. *I'm forgetting my own dictum. I shall say no more, save this: I feel that the conflicting elements of your soul will someday work out their differences, and balances will be redressed—or, should I say, imbalances will be corrected.*

"I'm all for it."

So, I will leave you. Farewell, Trent, my son. Believe me when I say you were my favorite.

He smiled and nodded. "I do, Mother. Farewell."

Her smiling image slowly faded. Before she disappeared completely, her small hand rose and slowly waved.

He sat alone and watched flames lick heat from the gray logs.

MINE

IN A SUBBASEMENT of the administration building they found a tunnel that led into the mine.

There was a huge metal door at the end of the tunnel and it looked impregnable.

"More magic?" Sativa asked.

"Sure. Always worth a try, but remember what I said about repeating spells. It wears them out. There should be enough left of the first one. I gave it all I had."

"That's a vanadium steel door with a tamper-proof lock. Can't be picked or probed."

"Oh, I dunno. Seems rather straightforward to me."

She grunted. "The only thing straightforward is—" Her jaw suddenly dropped.

Grinning, Gene swung the heavy door open. "Spell's working pretty good. If you hit it right, everything happens for you."

Sativa was thunderstruck. "But that's impossible. The combination to that lock is thousands of digits long. You couldn't possibly . . ."

"It opened by itself."

"How?"

"Uh, quantam tunneling. Little electrons just suddenly deciding to cross a resistor, all in the proper sequence."

"But the chances of that happening by accident are—"

"Vanishingly small. I know. But that's what a facilitation spell does, see. It makes the remotely possible very probable. As long as there's a chance that it could happen, it will happen. But as I said, you gotta do it just right. It doesn't always work."

Sativa shut her mouth and said no more.

They entered and Gene shut the thick door behind them. They now found themselves in a crossing tunnel and Gene motioned to the left, as stacked equipment lay in the shadows to the other side.*

The walls of the tunnel were metal, which led Gene to surmise that this was not the mine proper, but a passageway to the main shaft. He was proved right when they encountered a room like a hub, where several corridors converged, spokelike. At the center was a circular pillar into which was set a pair of wide doors looking not unlike those of a freight elevator.

"The glory-hole," Gene said.

"You mean the main shaft? Probably not. It may go all the way down to the haulage floor, but it's a lift, a way of moving equipment from level to level. The mining techniques here are sophisticated. Don't assume this is some open-cut operation."

"Don't know a thing about mining, really. Was just guessing."

"Guess away," Sativa said. "Meanwhile, we don't have a chance of getting into this lift."

---

*The author has never been in a mine, either, but read several books about mining. There is not far from his residence an abandoned coal mine, which belches smoke and flame occasionally. This might also be a classical reference.

"Maybe."

"The spell is still working?"

"Should be, but . . ." Gene thought it over. "Maybe I should goose it a little."

"You're the magician. Use your own judgment."

"Usually with me it's all judgment fled, and all that."

"I'm sorry."

"Never mind. Yeah, I think I'll kick it up a notch."

Gene rubbed his palms against his thighs, then shook his arms vigorously. He stepped his right foot back and assumed an odd stance, positioning his arms dramatically.

He gave Sativa a look. "Helps if you strike the proper wizardly pose."

"You look ridiculous."

"Thank you."

She was instantly regretful. "Forgive me." She laid an affectionate hand on his shoulder.

He nuzzled her hand, then went out of character to pull her close. They embraced and kissed.

When their lips parted, she smiled. "My wizard."

"Princess."

He let her go and she stepped back. He again assumed a melodramatically occult stance, somewhat akin to the manner of Bela Lugosi in his declining years.

He recited: "There once was a man from Khartoum, who took a lesbian up to his room . . ."*

Sativa laughed.

The curved elevator doors rolled aside with a hiss.

"Hey, that didn't take much goosing," he said.

The lift was empty. They entered.

---

*No, he's never been to Khartoum, either. In fact, he mostly sits home and reads a lot. Last year, in researching a novel, he read six books on the subject of golf. Imagine that.

"Something's bothering me," Sativa said as the doors closed.

"Yes?"

"Number of things, really. One, why doesn't the security system recognize us as intruders? Why hasn't it challenged us?"

"It's being fooled by the spell. Doesn't even know we're here, probably."

"I don't understand, but I'll take your word for it."

"What other thing is bothering you?"

"This is supposed to be a test facility. An abandoned one. But it looks too elaborate."

"Couldn't be a working mine with that administration building stripped."

"I suppose not. Unless the operation was being run clandestinely, from some other location. Underground or shielded."

"I don't get the sense of a working operation here."

Sativa sighed. "Neither do I, really. But I'm getting a strange feeling."

Gene looked at the control panel. It was lettered in strange script, but he got the gist. He punched the tab for a deep sublevel.

Machinery whined softly. The elevator lurched, then began to descend.

Sativa surveyed the space in which they stood.

"Roomy," she said. "Must have lots of heavy equipment here."

"If it's a test facility, maybe not. Just a means of getting drills and stuff from floor to floor, as you said."

"I suppose they load the stuff in from the level above the one we entered on."

"On the surface? I guess."

"Didn't see anything up there."

"Maybe another level. We're inside a mountain. Maybe a tunnel opens out somewhere else."

"Yes," Sativa said. "I saw a dried lake bed on the other side of this mountain. Good landing field. I didn't use it because it looked too obvious. But if you were delivering heavy equipment from orbit, that's where you would land."

The lift went down slowly but smoothly. At last it whined again, slowing until it dropped. A tone sounded and a glowing numeral appeared on a screen set into the panel.

"Here we are," Gene said. "Notions, lingerie."

"You're so very strange."

"Thank you kindly, princess. Which way?"

The tunnel ran to darkness in either direction.

"To the left," she said. "For no good reason."

"Good enough reason by me. Wait a minute." Gene studied the control panel.

"What do you want?"

"Want the doors to stay open. The spell might wear off, and . . ."

"A grounded lift might tip them off."

Gene scratched his stubbly chin. "You're right, of course. Wasn't thinking. But we'll be stuck down here if I can't get my mojo working."

"Your—"

"Talisman. No, we'll send it up."

"It's automatic."

"Right."

The closing of the doors left them in the faint greenish glow of the luminous strips on her pressure suit. There was enough light, however, by which to navigate the capacious, smooth-floored tunnel.

Sativa said, "Again, I'm puzzled by the extent of this operation. How many sublevels?"

"Seven marked on the panel, at least, but there were unmarked buttons."

"That's going fairly deep."

"And there could be some deeper."

"When do you think your magic spell will wear off?"

"Well, hard to say. We have maybe an hour."

"They we'd best get lost somewhere down here. Find a spot to hide, and stay there."

"There's a problem of food and water."

"Of course. We'll have to hold out as long as we can, then come back up when they give up looking."

"Are they likely to give up?"

She shook her head. "No. They know we're . . . Excuse me, they know *I'm* here. They won't stop till they've caught me."

"Then let's hope someone stashed some emergency rations in this hole. Mines are supposed to have that sort of stuff. Bottled water at least."

"There is that chance."

"Then that means we have a chance. Come on."

They walked into the semidarkness. Huge bracing trusses loomed overhead, looking secure enough to hold up the roof of a cathedral.

"You're right," he said, "it doesn't look like a quickie strip mine."

"It doesn't seem like a mine at all."

"What else could it be?"

"I don't know."

"What's this stuff?"

The stuff was piled crates lining the tunnel on both sides. The crates were made of some shiny white composite material.

Sativa knelt to inspect one of them. "They've got locks. Think you can handle it?"

"What, that thing?" He gave the crate a kick and the lid popped open.

Inside were futuristic firearms—rifles, or the equivalent. Sativa got one out and tore it free of its cloth wrapping. It was a formidable thing with a wire stock and a scope. She tossed it to him.

"Guns. Who—?"

"The Irregular Forces," she said. "This is one of their weapons caches."

"Gotcha. These could come in handy."

"Right," she said as she took out another weapon. "But this explains how we got in."

"It does?"

"Yes. No insult to your magical abilities, but we were obviously let in. A trap. That's why the outer door slammed shut."

"I see. But not necessarily true. My magic works, believe me. And it was working. I can tell."

"Let's hope you're right, my handsome wizard."

She got up and bussed him on the cheek.

"But let's look for ammunition, just in case."

"Check, princess."

RIVER

" . . . AND SO THE HOOKER SAID to the chicken, 'Sure, honey. Throw in a jar of mayonnaise and you got yourself a deal.' "

Full-throated laughter came from the stern of the ferry-boat, faint echoes returning from far across the water.

"That was amusing. Tell another."

The shore took form out of the darkness ahead. Bare but for a few quaint buildings hugging the edge of the water. Taken as a whole, the assemblage looked not unlike a fishing village. This was impossible.

"I have about exhausted my trove of conceits and epigrams," he told the boatman.

"Then spin me another tale of adventure."

"The shore nears."

The ferryman looked. "So it does. But you have given good measure. For the briefest moment I have been diverted from the tedium of my routine. And for that, mortal, I thank you."

"You are quite welcome, boatman. What is this place?"

"The Port of Dreams."

"Why is it so called?"

"I know not. Unlike the rest, you ask many questions. You will have your answer in due time."

He regarded the approach of the village, peering past the houses.

"This is an island?"

The ferryman nodded. "Aye."

"One more question, please. What is the name of this river?"

"This is the River of Dreams."

"Ah."

"And just downstream, at its mouth, begins the Sea of Oblivion, into which the river empties."

"I see. These names elicit in me a strange foreboding."

"Such feelings are often justified."

Ahead, a wooden dock. Along the shore the masts of many sailing ships reached up to the darkness overhead. He wondered how he could see anything in this gloom. But see he did.

The village seemed quite the going concern. Workers plied the docks, toting bundles. People in robes gathered along the shore in little groups, talking. Doing business, perhaps.

He again grew aware of his nakedness.

"Have you anything I might wear?" he asked the ferryman.

"Not I. But such may be purchased ashore."

Again, this purchasing. With what?

The ferryboat drew up to the dock and kissed its side. The boatman cast a mooring line. A barefooted dockhand caught it and tied it off.

He stepped from the boat to the dock and turned.

"My thanks."

"It is nothing. You tell good stories, mortal. Before I go, one more? A witticism, anything."

"A riddle?"

"A riddle then."

"Knock, knock."

"Who is there?"

"Not a soul."

The boatman regarded his passenger.

"You have given me something to think on, mortal. Fare thee well."

"Catch you later."

He watched the ferryboat pull away. Soon it vanished into the darkness whence it had come.

Looking down at his nakedness, he pondered what to do. He looked up. No one paid him the slightest mind. He shrugged. He began walking toward shore over the rough planks of the dock.

A man with a pushcart offered his wares.

"Garments, sir?"

He stopped. "Yes. But I cannot pay."

"Pity." The man pushed off.

He reached shore and walked left along the wharf, past docks that led out to tall ships. There were many, their riggings varied and exotic. He stopped to examine a particularly striking vessel.*

He realized that he was hungry.

How could this be?

Well, why not?

He looked around. There were shops, ship's chandlers for the most part. But he smelled food and followed the scent down a cobblestone street until he found himself in front of an inn. He entered.

---

*As you can see, the Greek mythology theme has been dispensed with in favor of more cryptic allusions. What he's getting at here is anybody's guess.

It was a small place, narrow and dark, with a sawdust floor. But the odors were good and the place had a pleasant atmosphere. A few tables were occupied; people sipping drinks and talking.

He approached the bar, where a man in rumpled robes was wiping glasses with a greasy cloth.

"I am in need of food and drink," he said.

The man looked up, the stub of a cigar clenched between his teeth.

"So?"

"I am willing to work for you. All I require in payment is some bread and a tumbler of water."

"Oh, really?"

"That is all."

"You want a job, that it?"

"Yes. I need a job. Temporarily."

"Yeah, it's always temporary. Until you get yourself a ship."

He realized it must be true. "Yes. That is correct."

"Yeah. Look, pal . . ."

The man plucked the fetid cigar stub from between his thin lips. "I got nothin' for ya. Business been slow. I don't know what it is, but it's been like a morgue around here lately. I got no need for a waiter, busboy, whatever. Okay, pal? Try up the street."

"I must get a ship."

"Yeah, I heard it all before. Your family was hard up, couldn't give you a decent burial. So you get here, butt hanging out, y'aint got a nickel, can't get arrested. Hey, I really feel for ya, pal, but like I said, I got nothin'."

"If you loan me some money, I will pay you back."

"What do I look like, a banker? You see any money-changers here? Hey, do yourself a favor. Go see Traveler's Aid. They'll help you out."

"I can entertain your customers."

"You go— Huh? What can you do?"

"I . . ."

"Yeah?"

"I can play the piano and tell jokes."

The man looked around. "Well, I'll just tune up the old Steinway. . . . Hey, you see a piano in here?"

"Get one."

The man guffawed. "You know what a—"

"Rent one. Lease one."

"You got all the answers."

"You said business was bad. Perhaps you need a draw."

The man was silent as he stuffed the cloth inside a beer mug and squeakingly wiped.

"Maybe you got an idea, there. Something to attract the walk-in trade. You play pretty good?"

"Fair. I tell good jokes. Patter. Satirical songs. One-liners."

"You got experience?"

"Plenty."

"OK. Let me ask around, see what rate I can get on an upright—"

"Baby grand would do better. You could position seats around it and I could take requests. You won't have to pay. I'll take the tips."

"Yeah. Lots of tips. I get seventy-five percent."

"I'll give you ten."

The man laughed toothily. "You'll hand over fifty percent and like it. I'm paying for the piano."

"We split sixty-forty, my favor."

The owner thought it over. "Okay, sixty-forty."

"And your cut gets cut to twenty-five after a month."

"There's no time here."

"Whenever."

"Minimum thirty."

"Done."

"Okay, pal, you got yourself a job. Here."

The man rolled a coin at him.

"Go out and get yourself some decent clothes. Don't want my employees walkin' around with their shortcomings exposed."

He took the gold coin. "Are you human?"

"Naw."

"But—"

"I like myself this way. Makes the mortals feel at home."

"Very well, then. I will be back."

"Wait." The owner pushed a tankard of ale across the bar. "You look like you need this."

He took the vessel and tilted it toward his mouth. He drank the whole thing down.

He wiped his mouth and caught his breath.

The owner grinned. "Yeah. Goes down good after a long ferry ride with that seven-foot-tall nightmare, huh?"

"Death's a bitch."

"And then you're reincarnated."

OFFICE OF THE REGENCY
(TEMPORARY QUARTERS)

"HELLO?"

"Am I speaking to His Excellency, the Regent?"

"You are."

"This is Giles, in the Ministry of Supply and Materiel."

"Yes, yes."

"Excellency, if I might have a word with you?"

"Yes! Go on."

"Those requisition forms you filed. Excellency, they weren't in proper format. Not only that, it was entirely the wrong form for such a requisition."

"So?"

"All requisitions must conform to procedure or they won't go through."

"So? Fix it so they do go through. I need that stuff."

"Begging your pardon, Excellency, but I can't touch them. It's against regulations."

"Hang regulations. Have one of your people do it."

"No can do, Excellency. Interoffice procedural regulations are quite specific. They don't quite have the force of statute law, but—"

"Oh, all right, send them back."

"I already did. This is a courtesy call. Please use the right form next time. For the materiel you're asking for, it's Office Supplies Requisition Form 1867 dash 401—"

"Wait! Damn it, this pen doesn't work."

"Yes, Excellency."

"Rupert! Gimme one of those . . . Right. Okay, what was that form number again?"

"Office Supplies Requisition Form 1867 dash 40178374 . . ."

"Right, right."

"Dash 2673 slash J."

" . . . 2673 dash J."

"No, *slash* J."

"Slash J. Right, got it. Will do."

"And they have to be signed by you personally."

"I did sign them! . . . Didn't I?"

"No, Excellency, the forms were rubber-stamped, by your secretary, I presume."

"Oh."

"That's no good for 2673 slash J. For any slash J form—you better write this down for future reference—any slash J form must be signed personally, not stamped . . . *and*—this is also very important—you must affix your seal of office."

"My goddamned seal of office hasn't come from the castle smithy yet."

"Well, that's a problem. In that case I'll have to have a sworn affidavit from you until you get the seal."

"Gods! All this for a damned box of paper clips?"

"Afraid so, Excellency."

"Amazing. Very well. Is that all?"

"Yes, Excellency. I'm truly sorry for any inconvenience."

"Forget it."

"But regulations . . . well, you know."

"I'm learning. Goodbye."

"Have a nice day."

Trent slammed the phone down.

"Rupert!"

The scribe came running back into the crypt, which had been hastily transformed into a working office.

"Excellency?"

"I need that damned seal. When?"

"It's on rush order. They said Monday at the earliest."

"Rats. Every damned form requires it. See if you can't rush them a little more."

"Yes, Excellency." Rupert wrote in a tiny notebook.

"What's next?"

"The Foreign Minister of Lytton is still waiting in the hall."

"Oh. Send him in."

"But the guild official has been waiting longer."

"What guild official?"

"The Castle Craftsmen's Guild, Excellency."

"Oh. I forgot. Well, send him in first."

"The Foreign Minister's the more important person. If you make him wait any longer it could be taken as a slight, and he might leave in a huff. Diplomatic incident. On the other hand—"

"Spill it."

"If the guild guy gets ticked off, he might just call a wildcat strike."

"Jeez, can he do that?"

"Well, sure."

"Get him in here."

The guild official was a burly fellow smoking a huge green cigar. He wore an expensive embroidered ministerial gown that did not quite hide his enormous gut. A red plume rose from his tricorn hat. He approached Trent's desk with a confident stride.

"Yes, sir, what can I do for you?" Trent said.

"You've had our grievance report for two weeks. We got nothing back from you."

"I hope you realize that I've been in office only a matter of days."

"I was speaking of the Administrative Offices. We want action on our grievance."

Trent shuffled papers around his desk. "Right. I can't seem to— *Rupert!*"

Rupert was brushing past the guild man with a file folder. "Excellency."

Trent took the folder and opened it. He glanced at the papers within.

"All right . . . uh, why don't you précis for me what exactly this is all about?"

"Hey, it's complicated. You shoulda read it."

"Sorry. Condense it."

"Actually, we're making some seniority adjustments. All we ask is that you go along with it and change your employee roster accordingly. Not much to ask . . . Excellency."

"So, what's the problem?"

"The problem is that Administration turned us down. We filed a grievance. You got it in your hand."

"Fine. Why are you making these adjustments—and when you say 'adjustments,' you mean what, exactly?"

"Demoting some employees to a lower seniority, is all."

"In favor of others, I assume?"

"Yeah, kinda."

"Why?"

"It's an internal matter. Guild business."

"So why come to us?"

"You gotta alter wage scales, benefits, schedules—"

"Who works and who doesn't, what they get paid."

"Yeah, you got it . . . Excellency."

"My brother turned you down, didn't he?"

"Yup."

"And you expect me to go against his wishes."

"You're in charge now, aren't you? The Council of Ministers—"

"No deal. I think I can intuit what's going on, and I don't like it. I don't like fiddling with a servant's livelihood unless there's a very good reason, and you've given me none."

"Like I said, it's internal. You can't interfere."

"I can refuse to act favorably on this grievance."

The guild man waved his cigar menacingly.

"And I can close this castle down."

"Get that weed out of my face, mister. I don't take kindly to threats."

"I can order a walkout any time," the guild official said casually, withdrawing the pungent cigar.

"Let me ask you a question. Why does it take no less than five footmen to attend a coach?"

"You got a problem with that?"

"Yes, I happen to have a problem with that. From now on three is the maximum."

"We got a contract!"

"I'm renegotiating, unilaterally, as it were."

"We'll walk!"

"Then walk."

"The funeral! You'll need—"

"Get out."

"But—"

"Out! And take that burning bush with you. You don't have the proper beatific mien for it."

Rupert shook his head as the guild official stalked out.

When the door slammed he said, "You handled that very badly, Excellency. If I may make so bold as to say."

"You just said it. Yeah, you're right. He really got my goat. I suppose I've bought myself a load of trouble."

"He not only controls the craftsmen—seamstresses, wainwrights and such—but teamsters and draymen as well."

"I know, I know. Okay, get the other guy in here. Ye flipping gods."

"Excellency, there are more visitors in the hallway—we really should get a proper anteroom—"

Trent groaned, wiping his forehead with a paisley handkerchief.

"Excellency?"

"Monster headache. I'll be all right. It's the goddamned banishment thing. I'll have to take a break at some point, get the hell out of the castle."

"Your schedule for the next few days is crammed. In fact, it's crammed into next week."

"To say nothing of the state funeral. That's got to last what, all day?"

"Most of the day, Excellency."

"Wonderful. With lugubrious music, too."

"His Majesty's tastes in music were good. The *Missa Solemnis* is scheduled."

"Oh. Well . . . Gods. Rupert, do you smoke? I need a cigarette."

"I wasn't aware that His Excellency—"

"I quit long ago, but this curse thing is driving me crazy. I need something, and alcohol won't do. With booze I'd just teleport right to cloud cuckoo land, nothing would get done."

"I can have someone run to the tobacconist."

"Fine. Let's see . . . oh, the guy from Lytton. By the way, where and what the hell is Lytton?"

"A kingdom in the Albion aspect. Much like England of Earth in the Elizabethan period."

"Okay, Rupert, show the fellow in. Oy."

"*Gevalt*," the secretary said, turning toward the door.

One after the other, visitors trooped in and out of the office: envoys, ambassadors, ministers plenipotentiary—diplomats of every sort, along with a *posse comitatus* of castle functionaries, each with their problems, grievances, petty squabbles, and sundry preoccupations.

The clock chimed nineteen times.

Trent looked up. "Ye gods and little pink elephants, look at the time."

Rupert closed the door on the clot of supplicants still in the hallway.

"No more, Rupert, I'm fagged out."

"The Regent's office is hereby closed for the day."

"Thank the deities."

Trent reached for the pack of cigarettes, found one crumpled, and lit it anyway. He took a long drag and sat back.

"I'm done in. Did Inky do this every single day?"

"This was a relatively slow day."

"You gotta be kidding me. I mean, there are only so many hours. Come on."

"Oh, he used magical coping methods, indubitably."

"I'd hate being forced into that. Not good to have a gaggle of spells going on at one time. It gets confusing and sometimes it's dangerous."

"His Majesty was a past master at that art."

"I know. 'Art' is the key word. I'm a good magician, but Inky had a certain style about him. He was a stylist. An artist. So am I, but some styles are better than others. Inky was great at subtle spell interaction."

"He was, Excellency. That he was."

Trent sighed. "Sometimes I lean toward acceding to the proposition that Inky was simply the better magician."

"His Excellency underrates himself."

"You're kind, Rupert. But I'm afraid it's true."

Trent took another long pull on the cigarette. He began a bout of coughing which threatened to turn into a fit.

Still hacking, he mashed the cigarette out in a clamshell ashtray. The tray flipped to the floor and smashed.

"Is His Excellency all right?" Rupert asked, bearing a glass of water.

Trent took it and drank. Recovered, he said, "Thanks. Ye gods, those frigging things can kill you!"

Rupert smiled.

"No more," Trent said firmly, throwing the rest of the pack of cigarettes into the trash can. "Enough of that. I'll never live my twenty-five score years and ten if I start smoking again."

"His Excellency makes a wise decision."

"Let's cut the 'Excellency' bit, all right? It's really starting to rankle. Makes me sound like I should be wearing a handlebar mustache and goatee."

"It is the proper honorific for your station."

"We'll have to do something about that. I'm still a prince of the realm, you know."

"Yes, sir."

"And maybe I should have stayed a prince."

Trent suddenly rose.

"Sir, are you leaving for the day?"

"I'm outta here. I'll be back tomorrow . . . I think."

"Excell—er, my lord prince. One more thing."

Trent was tying on his cape as he replied, "What is it now?"

"Just this report from the Royal Undertaker that I thought might not wait."

"What's it say?"

"It's sealed, my lord, and marked 'Confidential.' "

"Really? Let's have it."

Trent took the envelope from his side and ripped it open.

"Have no idea what the Royal flipping Undertaker would have to say that I—"

He read.

Rupert stood by, arms folded.

Trent lowered the sheet and stared off. Presently he said, "Holy smoke."

Rupert's eyes widened.

Trent looked at him. "Send a note to my wife. Won't be home for supper."

"Yes, my lord prince. Shall I say—?"

"I'm going to Malnovia."

Trent walked purposefully out of the crypt, slamming the door behind him.

Rupert looked around at the shambles the office had become, and sighed.

"What a flipping mess."

MINE

THEY FOUND ammunition in a crossing tunnel, and there was plenty of it, leading Sativa to speculate that the mine concealed one of the biggest Irregular Forces weapons caches along the Thread.

"They wouldn't use this good a hideout just to store slug throwers," she said.

"Slug throwers. Aren't these beam weapons?"

"No. Magnetically impelled projectile rifles. Standard close-combat weapons."

"Oh, well, I sorta thought, you know—ray guns."

"Ray guns? Oh, coherent-energy weapons? Spacecraft use them, of course. Do you realize how much raw power it takes to operate a typical particle-beam battery?"

"Not offhand."

"It draws from a string of nuclear pulse reactors hooked up in parallel."*

"Oh. No 'set phasers on stun' in this universe, eh?"

"Whatever that means."

*There is no such thing as a "nuclear pulse reactor." The author just made that up.

"So you think there're other sorts of arms here?"

"That's what I'm going to find out. Let's move."

"Rations, too, do you think?" Gene asked hopefully as he trotted after her.

"Certainly."

"Then we could hole up here quite a while. This place is cavernous."

"I can't do that. I must find some way back to the Dominion and report this. It's my duty."

"Right."

The mine was cool and extremely dry; perfect storage conditions. They discovered more military equipment, tons of it: guns, ammunition, artillery rounds, missiles, and other weapons Gene had trouble identifying. Some things seemed to be light artillery, mortars and such. Other stuff Sativa identified as "smart" mines (capable of distinguishing friend from foe), "electrogravitic" field generators, and "friendly" bombs. (What these last were capable of he never found out. Maybe, Gene thought, they took their targets to lunch before blowing them up.)

Many of these weapons had miniature nuclear warheads, some with yields as low as .01-kilotons—more simply, equivalent to 10 tons of high explosive.

"The big weapons are probably on another level," she conjectured.

"Big nukes?"

"Large-yield fusion and fission devices, surely. But I'm talking about singularity devices."

"I *think* I can grasp what those might be."

"Planet-breakers."

"That's what I was afraid of."

"Never been used in actual warfare, but they've been tested."

"Wait till Greenpeace hears about this."

"What?"

"Never mind. What do you want to do? Go back to the surface?"

"The only chance we have is to try to steal one of their ships."

"No. The only chance we have is getting back to the castle."

"Whatever are you jabbering about?"

"I'm talking about finding the interdimensional gateway between this world and the one I came from. Actually, it's not a matter of finding it—I know where it is. The trick would be getting there without getting blasted or picked up."

Sativa stared at him for a moment. "You *are* serious about this."

"Absolutely. I don't have a ship."

"And this . . . gateway. It's some sort of spacetime anomaly?"

"You could think of it as such. Yes."

"And there's magic involved?"

Gene sighed. "Look, I've never been able to understand it myself. The castle is a huge source of power. I've been given to understand that this power has its source in something supernatural. Beyond that, I really don't know much. All I know is it works. I can get you out of here. We can return to my world for a while until the coast is clear. Then you can come back here and either repair your ship or get that super-radio in the administration building working, so you can send for help. How does that sound to you?"

"Fantastic."

"I don't think you mean 'wonderful.' You mean you can't believe it. Right?"

"I think the whole notion is a fantasy. I think you're

balmy. I think *I'm* balmy. I'm really dreaming this—still back there pinned in that wreckage."

"No, you're not."

Gene slung his futuristic rifle over his shoulder.

"Let's get up to the surface," he said.

"First let's load up with whatever we can find in the way of advantages down here."

"More guns?"

"Grenades, maybe a hand missile-launcher."

"Good idea."

They rummaged through the crates until they found such. The grenades were unbelievably small, little more than the size of golf balls. To arm them, one simply pushed in an easy-to-push tab.

"Isn't that dangerous?"

"They know when and when not to go off."

He did a double take. "Huh? How could—?"

"They're very aware. They can read your emotional states, the surroundings."

"I don't get it."

"And they just won't go off near the hand that arms them."

"No kidding. What *will* they think of next."

Brilliant missiles, apparently. She showed him how to work the launcher. The missiles themselves were miniature, yet carried a fission micro-warhead.*

"I don't believe it. I just can't believe these are nukes."

"Just barely. Cobalt core, barely explodes at all."

"Oh, well, cobalt . . ."

The launcher was ultralightweight and could be carried strapped across the back. From what Sativa hastily ex-

---

*Say, this is nice. I mean, talking like this. You strike me as very intelligent, warm, and sensitive; fun to be with.

plained, he gathered that aiming was automatic, and that the missile could maintain its own course—not trajectory, as it was more or less a cruise missile—stay on target, and make corrections for evasive action along the way. And do all brilliantly.

"Not bad for a Mattel toy," he said, which was exactly how the whole affair struck him.

"I'm going to stop asking about these obscure allusions of yours. You've convinced me that you're from another world. No one would go to all that trouble making up background detail."

They moved off into the darkness, heading back the way they had come, toward the freight elevator. On the way, Gene still marveled at the detail his eyes now picked out, the massiveness of the overhead trusses, the level floor, the way rock was sheared clean and smooth, the general cleanliness of the place. The design seemed to preclude the usual dangers associated with mining: cave-in, explosion, and lethal gases. The whole operation seemed to say, very clearly: SAFETY FIRST.

Now, had the Irregulars done most of this, or was the mine intended to be this way? He inclined toward the latter possibility. It looked like a mine, not just a storage facility. There were many more tunnels and shafts than a mere underground warehouse would warrant, most of them empty. No, it would not be wise of the Irregulars to put all their explosive eggs in one basket. The mine preexisted; the rebels were only squatters.

He was about to comment on all of this, when Sativa suddenly halted and he had to skid on the linoleum-like floor to keep from colliding with her.

"What—?"

Her hand shot up to muffle him.

She whispered in his ear, "I heard something."

They retreated.

Soon, at their backs came voices. Barked orders. Echoing footsteps.

Turning left at the next crossing tunnel, they hurried along as fast as they could, passing stacks of crates. They made another turn farther along, then were faced with a decision: Go toward the central shaft, into the thick of their pursuers, or away, toward a possible and even probable cul-de-sac.

They chose the dead end.*

*Would you like to get together for lunch someday?

PORT OF DREAMS

"SO, WHAT HAPPENS OUT THERE on the Sea of Oblivion?"

The place was full, though the patrons were subdued, as usual. Smoke drifted ceilingward. Hushed conversations, except for the one between two men at the piano bar.

Glasses tinkled as the piano player did a soft, slow rendition of "These Foolish Things."

"Nobody knows," said the other barfly. "No one's ever come back from the Sea."

"Yeah? I need another drink. I don't like this being dead business."

"So what's to like? It's the way things are, my friend. You pays your money and you takes your chance."

"I still don't like it. I bought my boat today. Those chandlers charge an arm and a leg to outfit a boat."

"Ship."

"Whatever. Anyway, I ship out tomorrow, on the tide."

"Time and tide. Good luck."

"Hey, are you supposed to say that? I mean, isn't it bad luck to wish a sailor good luck?"

"That's actors."

"Oh. Actors. I hope I make it back. Kinda like it here."

"It's just a way station, they say."

"Wish it wasn't. Wish we could just settle down right here, open up a nice little business, something like this tavern. Hire a piano player, like this guy."

"He's pretty good."*

"Yeah, he is. Hey, buddy, you're a pretty good piano player, you know that?"

"Thanks."

"Yeah. Here's something for ya."

A gold coin tinked into the tumbler on the baby grand.

"Thank you, sir."

"Don't mention it, pal. Don't mention it. Hey, where I'm going, who needs money?"

The other barfly said, "You need it to get where you're going."

"Hey, that's true. You die without the cash, you're up the creek without a paddle."

"Or up the river."

"Yeah, and you need to get down the river."

"On the other hand, if you get sold down the river, you might wind up up the creek without a paddle."

The first barfly burst into laughter.

"Hey, that's pretty good. That's funny. Hey, piano player, wasn't that a great gag? Huh?"

"Yes, sir, sure was funny."

"You're too kind. Why the hell am I making jokes, though? I wish someone could tell us what the hell *is* out there on the Sea Of Oblivion. At least we'd know what we're in for."

---

*I hope you don't think me forward. We're getting along so swimmingly. Do you read much? I do. What kind of music do you like? I go for a little classic rock, some contemporary, a little jazz, and Baroque. . . . Oops, sorry, have to go back to work. Talk to you later.

"Who wants to know? What good would it do if we did know?"

"I'd feel better, somehow, knowing."

"Like you said, it's inevitable. You pays your money, and like that."

Conversation continued. Before long the piano player launched into "You Belong to Me."*

The two barflies listened.

"I never saw the pyramids."

"Neither did I. What the heck are pyramids?"

"I guess we're not from the same world."

"Nah, I guess not."

"I wonder if there's more than one afterlife."

"Huh?"

"If there are many worlds—and I hear there are indeed a shitload of them—I wonder if there aren't a whole assortment of different and differing afterlives. Maybe this is just one of a number of possible ones."

"Hey, that's interesting."

"Just idle speculation."

"What do you think about that, piano player, huh?"

"Sir, I think the gentleman is right."

"Hey, what do you think of that? Maybe in some afterlives, you get everything free. I'm all for that."

"But here money is a token of moral worth, my friend."

"Is *that* why I got here so poor? I coulda sworn I socked away enough for a better ship than the one I got."

"It means your life didn't amount to all that much, friend. Just like most folks. You left the world you lived in more or less the way you found it, neither better nor worse for your having been there."

---

*The author would have quoted some lyrics, but obtaining the proper rights and permissions is a costly and vexing process.

"Hey, I did okay."

"Not saying you didn't. Just saying you're an average guy, like me."

"Yeah, that's me. Average. I like it that way."

"Nothing wrong with it. Now, take our friend, here, the piano player. He brings music to the world."

"This ain't the world."

"The netherworld, whatever it is. He creates a little beauty, makes people happy. That's something. Me, I couldn't play 'Chopsticks.' No talent for anything."

"I thought you said you were a businessman."

"Yep, but I didn't show any particular talent for that either. I just got by."

"Hey, buddy, that's all you can expect. Just to get by."

"But it's all over, now. All over."

"Don't go sappy on me. Come on, drink up. I'll buy you another."

"Thanks. Let's buy the piano player a drink. Whaddya say?"

"Sure. Here, pal."

Two more gold coins plunked into the tumbler as the piano player finished the tune and did a short finale.

Scattered applause.

He rose from the keyboard and picked up the tumbler.

"Thank you, gentlemen. Much appreciated."

"Don't mention it, pal."

He made his way past the bar, nodding to the barkeep, Rhadamanthus, en route.

He found the owner, Minos,* in the back room, sitting at his untidy desk and writing in a ledger. Minos looked up, smiled, and laid down his pen.

---

*Cf. "Rhadamanthus," above. Note the return to mythology here. This mixing of ancient and modern allusions is very clever.

"Good crowd tonight, eh?"

"Pretty good. Drunker than usual, and all the more generous."

"That's the idea, pal. Part those fools from their cash."

"Here's your cut for the night. That was the last set."

Minos looked at his pocket watch. "Hey, look at that, almost closing time."

"Speaking of time, mine here is nearing its end."

"How long's it been?"

"Seventy years."

"That all? Seems like you've always been around. So, you got your nest egg up to respectable proportions, eh?"

"More or less. I have my eye on a sleek little schooner down at Alecto Wharf."

"So, you're gonna ship out at last, huh. Good luck. Talked with a chandler yet?"

"Not yet, but I have friends, connections."

"Outfitting'll set you back some, you know that."

"I know it. I have it all scoped out."

"Good, good."

Minos yawned and stretched his chubby arms.

"I'm bushed. Going to call it a night."

"Night, boss."

"G'night, Steve."

Minos paused at the door and said, "Your own name come to you yet?"

"No. I still go by 'Steve Daedalus'* around town."

"It'll come. Part of the learning process."

"Boss, what is it I'm supposed to be learning?"

"You got me, Steve. Not my department."

"I still have the vague feeling that I don't belong here."

---

*Again with the Greek stuff, this time by way of Joyce, which makes the allusion not only charming but adds layers of meaning as well.

"Yeah, you've said that many times. You know, I'm inclined to agree with you. You don't seem like the rest."

"I don't feel dead."

"Well, there's always some residual disbelief."

"I feel it's a lot more than that. I really do not believe I'm supposed to be here."

Minos shrugged. "But you're here. Hey, what are you gonna do? Maybe you just haven't faced facts yet."

"Possibly. Possibly."

"Then again . . ." Minos heaved his shoulders again. "I dunno. Maybe you'll find your answer out to sea, like everybody else. Maybe your case is special, but your destiny is still the same. The only way to find out is to get on that boat and take the final journey."

"To where, boss? Where?"

"But . . . Stevie boy, that's the whole point, isn't it?"

Steve nodded. "Yeah, I guess it is."

"Right. Well, I'll see you . . . Uh, you are gonna work one more shift?"

"Sure. Tomorrow-which-is-meaningless-here."

"Okey-doke. See you around."

"Right."

Minos shut the door after him.

He poured himself two fingers of ambrosia from Minos' hidden stash and sat, sipping thoughtfully.

Spot Quiz No. 2

Multiple Choice. Circle the correct answer.

1. A spell that makes things happen is called a:

   A. magic spell
   B. make-it-happen spell
   C. facilitation spell
   D. bribe

2. A device for faster-than-light communication is a:

   A. cellular phone
   B. CB radio
   C. multiphone
   D. friend of your wife

3. What character in Greek mythology does the strange specter in the ferryboat evoke?

   A. Charon
   B. Theseus
   C. Bellerophon
   D. Biff the Wonder Clam of Phrygia

4. Departed relatives may be contacted in the afterworld through the services of a:

   A. psychic medium
   B. necromancer
   C. good lawyer
   D. yenta

5. There once was a man from Khartoum, who took a lesbian up to his:

   A. room
   B. pad
   C. flat
   D. roommate

6. Life's a bitch, and then you:

   A. get transferred to New Jersey
   B. get audited by the IRS
   C. die and *then* get transferred to New Jersey
   D. die and *then* get audited by the IRS

7. *Posse comitatus* is a Latin phrase meaning:

   A. a band of unconscious deputies
   B. an unconscious pussycat
   C. a band of communist deputies
   D. a band of communist pussycats

8. If a .01-kiloton warhead can kill 1000 people, how many times more powerful would a warhead have to be in order to kill all the lawyers in the world?

   A. 100 times
   B. 1000 times
   C. 10,000 times
   D. nuclear weapons aren't that powerful

9. Author is to publisher as helpless swimmer is to:

   A. poisonous jellyfish
   B. riptide
   C. shark
   D. tidal wave

10. Book reviewer is to snake as literary critic is to:

   A. jerk
   B. weasel
   C. alcoholic failed writer with two divorces under his belt
   D. shithead

   Essay Questions. Again, your answer should be limited to 500 words.

1. Discuss the problems inherent in the task of adapting this novel as (1) a screenplay; (2) a radio drama; (3) a "graphic novel" (comic book); (4) a set of collector dinner plates.

2. Briefly outline the eschatologies of the world's major religions and compare and contrast them. Tell how you

wouldn't be caught dead in any of them, and are they kidding or what?

3. Write an essay praising the author in the most enthusiastic terms and send it to the publisher, along with an order for 15 copies of each of his books.

Suggested Projects:

1. Organize a jousting tournament in your neighborhood. Seek federal funding. The departments of Housing, Education and Welfare would be good places to start.

2. Organize a toad-fling in your neighborhood. Call it "performance art" or "conceptual art." Seek federal funding. The National Endowment for the Arts would be a good place to start.

MALNOVIA—ELECTOR'S PALACE
OFFICE OF THE CHAMBERLAIN

"SO KIND of you to pay us this visit, my lord."

The Chamberlain was an elderly man with a shiny bald pate and skin like wrinkled parchment. His eyes were sharp, his fingers long and thin. The office in which he sat was a rococo wonder, glinting with gold leaf on fancy scrollwork.

The chamber's high, mullioned windows looked out on an expanse of formal garden. The weather was sunny and pleasant, matching the Chamberlain's official disposition.

Nevertheless, Trent caught the hint of a nervous chill underneath all the diplomacy.

"Something of urgency came up," Trent said. "I came as soon as I could. You're very kind to receive me on such short notice, Chamberlain."

Trent's host raised both hands. "How could I refuse the brother of our late lamented Court Magician? What with the press of duties attending upon the funeral and other matters, I naturally assumed any request for a visit from a member of the family to be extremely urgent indeed."

"It is."

A servant came in, bearing a tray with a cut-glass decanter and long-stemmed glasses.

"Will you take some dry sack this afternoon, my lord?" the Chamberlain asked.

"Thank you."

Wine poured and served, the servant left, closing tall doors behind him. The sound echoed in the high chamber.

"And now, my good lord," the Chamberlain said, "would you be so kind as to tell me what brings you to our fair principality?"

Trent set his glass down on a small table at this side.

"I have reason to believe that my brother was murdered."

After helping to sop up the wine that the Chamberlain had sprayed and spilled across the desk, Trent sat back down. He waited for the Chamberlain to stop choking.

At last, hoarse-voiced and weakly smiling, the Chamberlain said, "Went down the wrong pipe, that did."

"Very sorry to be so brusque."

"Think nothing of—" The Chamberlain coughed, took a gulp of sherry, coughed once again and cleared his throat. He then went on: "Whatever makes you think that your brother was—" He swallowed hard. "Murdered?"

"One thing only. There is some sort of spell on him. A very subtle and hard-to-detect spell. And in fact it was only detected when the undertaker tried to cast a preservation spell on the body. The spell was warded off by something."

The Chamberlain finished mopping the desk with is handkerchief and sat back. "This is very interesting. Uh . . . but of course, your brother was a magician. Could this spell be of his doing?"

"No. It is not his style."

"I'm not sure I—"

"Each magician has his own, identifiable style, like an

artist. It's as unmistakable as a signature. I know my brother's hand, and this spell is not his work."*

"I see. Yes, I've heard that about magic and magicians."

"It takes some sensitivity to perceive these subtleties, naturally."

"Naturally. Doubtless you know whereof you speak."

The Chamberlain drained his glass and poured himself another from the decanter.

He sat back, glass in hand. "Now, exactly, what is it you want of me?"

"I want an investigation, naturally."

"An investigation? Ah, yes . . . yes."

"I want the murderer brought to justice. To do that, you have to catch him—and to do *that* you must proceed with the usual police procedures. You—" Trent leaned forward. "Unless there's some problem with that?"

"Problem. Well, I actually can't say at the moment. I see no reason why there would be any difficulty, looking at it at first blush. Of course, if there's been a *murder*, why it follows as the night the day that . . . uh, well—"

Trent slumped back. "I take it there is some problem."

The Chamberlain drank and set the glass on his sedulously polished desk. "I suppose it would be better to say that I see no barrier to our proceeding with a murder investigation, or any criminal investigation, provided I can present the Lord Prosecutor's office with clear prima facie evidence of criminal wrongdoing."

"In other words, you're saying my word isn't good enough."

---

*Very clever notion. This novel is rife with clever notions. At times it borders on being too clever by half. But at least it is not a dull book. There is quite a good deal of dull stuff being published these days in the fantasy genre. Droves of dragons, Celtic swordswomen, elves, magic blades, and the rest, all with titles like *Swordwanker*, *Witchflinger*, *Dragonsdong*, *Dragonwhacker*, *Spellmacher*, and worse. Honestly, it's enough to make you puke into your flagon of mead.

The Chamberlain raised a hand in protest. "My lord, I say no such thing. I have no reason to doubt you. But I can't approach the Lord Prosecutor with anything but hard evidence. Not necessarily conclusive evidence, mind you, but evidence of some kind other than the conjecture, however well-founded, of an aggrieved relative, even one of so high a station as yourself."

"I see. What sort of evidence would you need?"

"The usual, my lord. First and foremost, clear forensic proof that death was caused by occult means."

"Very hard to get."

"Indeed, indeed."

"What else?"

"Well, again, the usual sorts of things. Depositions of eyewitnesses."

"Again, difficult in magical cases."

"Evidence of the means by which the murder was committed."

"Tough."

"A motive—"

"Means, motive, and opportunity, the whole bit."

"Precisely, my lord. Solid forensic proof would be enough to start things off."

"Well, I'll see if that can't be done, somehow," Trent said. "Should be some way, though I don't know much about these things. I'll talk to Dr. Mirabilis. Our forensic pathologist."

"Would he be able to detect another hand in the spell and file a deposition to that effect?"

"Possibly." Trent reached for his glass. "Damn it, I don't know. He's good at medical magic and not much else."

"Ah," the Chamberlain said regretfully. "Then . . ."

"I'm up shit creek without a kayak."

"I beg your pardon?"

"Nothing. Is there any way . . . What if I speak to the Lord Prosecutor himself? If I could convince him—"

"I am afraid that his lordship is away on state business. He won't be back for several weeks."

"Well, that's no good. My brother will be in his grave. It will be hell persuading my people to exhume the body."

The Chamberlain sighed. "Well, I suppose there's nothing to be done."

"Perhaps the Prosecutor can be reached by messenger?"

"Yes, but it would be several days getting word back, and I'm afraid it would be difficult for his lordship to initiate a major criminal investigation at such a great remove."

"Nevertheless, I must give it a try. Would you have your secretary draft a message for me? I'll dictate."

The Chamberlain seemed hesitant. "Why, of course."

"Where is the Prosecutor, by the way?"

"With the Emperor."

Trent's shoulders sagged. "No doubt he's preoccupied."

"Oh, very much so, my lord. He's assisting in an investigation of high crimes and misdemeanors among His Imperial Majesty's own ministers. His time will be at a premium. I said that it would take a few days for him to respond. I should have added that a few weeks might be the more likely interval."

"Great."

"Eh? Oh. Yes, unfortunate. And, of course . . ."

Trent's blue eyes narrowed. "Yes?"

"Well, you know, magicians."

"What about magicians?"

The Chamberlain shrugged. "No one likes to meddle in these things. This city is full of magicians. They practically have their own government. The Magicians' Guild is powerful. Most of time they dispose of these matters among themselves, and no one gainsays them the right to do it."

"So," Trent said. "I must deal with them."

"So it would seem. Have you any connections here?"

"None. I haven't been here in . . . well, it's been quite a while."

"I would recommend visiting the local chapter of the Guild."

Trent was silent as he stared out the window.

"I am very sorry, my lord, that I have nothing else to offer. Would you . . . would you care for more sherry?"

Trent's answer was slow to come. "Hm? Oh. No, no thank you. I shall be leaving, Chamberlain."

Trent rose and gathered up his cape.

The Chamberlain rose with him. He was a small man, eager to please, fearful of giving offense, politic in the extreme, and totally bland.

"Thank you so much, Chamberlain."

"It is nothing, my lord. What will you do?"

"I will stay in Malnovia, for the moment, if the Elector will permit."

"I shall see that you are granted every amenity."

"My thanks."

"But what else will you do, my lord?"

"I shall try to find my brother's murderer."

The Chamberlain's expression was pained. "But are you *quite* sure he was murdered?"

"Very sure."

"But, my lord, isn't it sometimes better not to meddle where there is no hope of success? You are a stranger here. The chances you will uncover anything—please forgive— are quite remote. Why must you—?"

"I must," Trent said. "I must find out who killed Incarnadine—or else . . ."

"Yes?"

"They'll blame it on me."

Trent walked out of the high, resplendent chamber, his footsteps echoing hollowly.

CASTLE—CHAPEL

THE CHAPEL'S ARCHITECTURE was not truly Gothic, though it evoked the style. The castle's architecture was *sui generis,* * unique; but it did have second cousins, and one of them was Earth medieval.

Linda stared up at the ribbed vaulting of the roof, a roof that looked twenty stories high. "Chapel" was a misnomer. "Cathedral" was more like it, clerestory windows and all.

But this was not a Christian church. Linda had only a vague idea of the religion of the castle's world, knowing only that it was polytheistic and complex. But there weren't any statues here. No nine-armed gods, no scared bulls, none of the trappings of paganism, or what she thought of as paganism. Instead, the pillars, buttresses, and walls were covered with all manner of cryptic signs and symbols graven into stone.

Up front, there where the altar should have been but wasn't, Incarnadine lay in state, his body draped in robes, his face serene. The simple coffin was of dark wood, borne

*A Latin phrase for a farmer who raises pigs and overfeeds them.

on a bier of polished gold. The cathedral was hung with black shrouds. No flowers.

He doesn't look dead, she had thought when first viewing the body. *He can't be dead. He looks exactly as he did in life.* Slyly handsome, prominent chin, thick dark hair, fair complexion, thin nose. Robust, full of life.

She realized that she was in love with him.

He can't be dead. He can't be.

She had cried a lot over the last two days. She had to face reality. He was gone, forever. He had lived 300 years and more, and now he lived no longer. As strong as his magic was, it could not ward off the hex that afflicts all living things: the curse that says, *You must die.*

The scent of incense drifted to her. The place smelled like a church. Soft music was playing, emanating from an unseen speaker, she presumed. It sounded like strings, but she couldn't identify the kind of music it was, much less the selection.

She settled back in her seat and sighed. The place had no pews, just like the great medieval cathedrals. Chairs—quite comfortable ones—had been set up, and for them she was grateful.

No, actually the chapel didn't seem so much like a church after all. It was too much like the rest of the castle, and the castle was unlike anything on Earth. She wondered if Incarnadine had been a religious man. Did he believe in his family's traditional religion? Were there gods, real gods, in this universe? Everything else of a supernatural bent existed in this universe, and she decided that mere gods shouldn't be an exception.

She thought about her own views on religion. They didn't amount to much. She held very few firm convictions about anything important: religion, politics, philosophy. This lack had always bothered her.

She simply wasn't any kind of super-intellectual. Never had been. Gene—now there was a smart kid.

Too smart, sometimes. He was always thinking, furiously thinking, wheels turning, scheming.

Gene. Where the heck was he, anyway? A few servants had fanned out to look for him, but he was nowhere to be found. Off in some wild aspect, probably, having fun. Well, he was in for quite a shock when he came back. Incarnadine would be in his tomb by then.

The funeral was tomorrow. They'd moved it up. Incarnadine was supposed to have lain in state for a week or more, but somebody had second thoughts and rescheduled the service for tomorrow morning. Why, she didn't know.

She grew aware that other people had come into the chapel. She looked back to see Dalton, Thaxton, Deena Williams, and Melanie McDaniel heading her way, all wearing black armbands.

Linda was wearing a mourning outfit that she had whipped up. Black tights, a nice doublet with black sequins, black boots.

Dalton took the seat to her left, Melanie opposite.

"How are you holding up?" Dalton whispered.

"Fine."

Melanie asked, "Have you been eating?"

"Not really."

"You should."

"I know. I just don't have any appetite."

"You're taking this the hardest of all of us," Dalton said.

Linda heaved a sigh. "He just seemed to hold this whole world together. Without him, it's all like a crazy dream."

"I know what you mean."

"It's always seemed like a dream to me," Melanie said.

"But even here," Dalton said, "death is a fact of life."

"Yeah, it's so inevitable."

Thaxton leaned over to say, "I'm told the funeral will be quite a big do."

"Should be a real pageant," Dalton speculated.

"I hate funerals," Deena Williams said.

"Who likes them?" Melanie asked.

"I get all depressed."

"Wonder why."

"And I never liked church either."

"Well . . ."

"There's going to be an orchestra, I hear," Dalton said, craning his neck. "Back there in the choir loft, I guess. Mozart, Beethoven, and a bunch of stuff from other worlds by composers I've never heard of."

"He liked music," Linda commented.

"He was a singular man," Dalton said. "With all his powers, his gifts, it's hard to believe he was only human. There was something of the demigod about him."

"I never thought of him as godlike," Linda said. "He was human to me."

"Well, you're a great magician. You and he had something in common. You both could handle the castle's magic."

"I'm hardly in his league."

"Maybe not, but you're up there."

They all sat silently for a moment, listening to the strangely lilting strings.

"I can't figure out whether that music is tonal or atonal," Dalton said.

"Damned lugubrious," Thaxton opined.

"It's positively funereal."

Thaxton eyed him. "That's one," he said menacingly.

"Shhhh!"

The two former golfers looked back at Deena.

"Y'all ought to be ashamed of yourself."

"You always get me into trouble," Dalton whispered.

Chastened, they sobered up and were silent.

Presently Linda rose.

"You're right, I should eat something. I think I'm actually hungry now."

"I'll go with you," Melanie said.

"If you want. After, I'm going to rest up for the funeral. It's going to be a strain."

"You better believe it. This place will be packed."

"Yeah. On second thought, I'm just going to have supper served in my room. I'm tired. Gonna sack out till tomorrow. See you guys later."

They all nodded. Linda began the long walk to the door, her boots clacking against hard flagstone.

"Family been here?" Dalton asked Melanie.

"Yeah, they were here earlier. I went up to pay my condolences. Are you going to?"

"Never met them. Kind of awkward, but I should, I suppose."

"Well, of course you should, old man," Thaxton said. "Only proper."

"Yes. I will. This is all so damned bloody awful. What will we do without him?"

"At least we know Trent is a good guy," Melanie said.

The erstwhile duffers exchanged looks.

Dalton said, "He's not Incarnadine."

Shaft

"HERE IT IS!"

Gene had hoped that mining engineers so bent on safety would have thought of providing escape shafts in case of accident. Shafts that went all the way to the surface. They had indeed provided them.

He pushed against the panic-bar and the heavy blastproof door gave. He stepped halfway in and confronted a small landing which abutted a spiral stairway constructed of unpainted metal. The shaft was lit with tiny blue lights glowing dimly.

"This is convenient."

Sativa poked her head in and looked up and down the shaft.

"We're near the bottom level. It's a long way up."

They entered the shaft. Gene closed the door quietly. They then began a cautious climb up the spiral.

"I don't like the idea of being trapped between levels," he said in low tones.

"It's a chance we must take. Do you think it goes all the way to the surface?"

"Stands to reason. Opens out onto the slope of the hill, probably."

"Damn it," she said. "This is no good."

"Why?"

"They'd be fools not to cover all the safety exits."

He stopped. "Right. Should have thought of that." He thought a moment. "We could try to shoot our way out."

She shook her head. "You'd be killed. Let's explore the next level down. There is one entrance they might not cover."

"Which is?"

"The tunnel leading out to the plain."

"The one they use as a loading dock? We don't know if it really exists."

"It must. It's the only way to get anything big into the mine."

"But why wouldn't they be guarding that, too?"

"Because it's a hidden entrance and the inner door is probably huge and impregnable. But we can blast through it from this side."

"With the nukes? Jeez. Okay, I'm game. But which level?"

"We'll have to try them all. But my instincts say down."

"Right."

They reversed direction, increasing their pace a bit, trying to keep the stairway from vibrating with their footsteps. The walls of the shaft were of striated rock, smoothly bored. Gene wondered what high-tech marvel had sliced through solid rock like so much cheese. Lasers, probably, but maybe something better. Particle beams. Gamma-wave lasers?

Another landing below. Gene descended the last few steps and approached the door cautiously. He put his ear to it.

Sativa stood behind him and waited.

He took his time. At last he straightened up and looked at her.

"I'm going to risk a peek."

He grasped the handle, pressed the thumb tab, and pulled. He eased the door out of its jamb until a crack of darkness appeared. A draught of cooler air flowed to his face.

He listened. Then he widened the crack a hair and peeked.

The tunnel was empty except for more crates of armaments. He heard nothing. After waiting at least a quarter-minute, he opened the door and stepped out. He raised his weapon.

"Are you sure you can use that thing?" she asked.

"Are you sure you're a good teacher? I pushed all the right buttons."

"But the safety's on."

He glanced down. "Oh." He flipped the tiny lever the other way. "Thanks."

"Think nothing of it. Which way, do you think?"

"My sense of direction is fairly good. I'd say the other side of the mountain is to the left."

"Check."

Gene shut the door carefully, and darkness, except for Sativa's greenish glow, returned.

She touched something on her suit and the light cut out. They stood in complete darkness for a time, listening.

Silence.

Before long the strips along the front of her suit began glowing again.

"There is a proper light on this thing," she said. "But I've been reluctant to use it."

An intense beam shot from the region of her right shoulder and made a tight circle on the wall. She fiddled with a control until the circle widened.

"Little photon-shooter. I shouldn't be doing this, though." She shut it off. "Their sensors can pick up the tiniest bit of trace radiation."

The intensity had hurt Gene's eyes, and now the light's absence blinded him. But his heightened sensitivity returned quickly and soon he was navigating quite well by the weak halo of the strips.

More war materiel. These crates were bigger and there seemed to be more of them.

They walked on, carefully checking all directions at each intersection. Gene imagined himself having a sixth sense, sending out feelers into the darkness. It wasn't magic—he hadn't a magic spell for that—but he hoped there were enough remnants of the facilitation spell to give his imaginings some force. Nothing tickled his feelers yet, but he was getting a tingly feeling from them.

He stopped.

"Did you hear something?" He looked back.

"Um, no. Did you?"

"I thought."

They waited briefly, ears cocked.

"Must have kicked a pebble or something," he said.

They moved on.

Sativa pulled him close and whispered, "We'd better keep our voices down."

"Right, sorry."

Their footsteps were oddly muffled in the silence. Porous rock absorbing sound? Perhaps it was the kind of absolute silence that is overwhelmed by the body's own interior noise: heartbeat, the rush of blood, the creak of bone. The same way that the mine's utter darkness revealed spectral shapes and flashes—the random, stray firing of light-receptor cells in the retina.

It was not long before they heard a rumbling sound nearby, as of huge doors rolling back.

Sativa grabbed his arm and squeezed.

They retreated from the sound of the freight elevator, retracing their steps. They reached the door of the escape shaft. Gene opened it.

There came sounds of voices below. From high above, the unmistakable vibrating thud of heavy boots on the stairs.

"We're stuck, unless we find another shaft," he said. "Looks like we're going to be making that desperate last stand you mentioned."

They ran off into the darkness, made a few turns, and raced down a tunnel.

Another dead end. They skidded to a stop.

"You can give yourself up," Sativa said.

"So they can thank me and then kill me?"

"There's the chance they'd let you go."

"Back to my magic kingdom? Yeah, they'd believe that, all right."

"If it's real," she said, "you could prove it."

"I don't want them in my world. Besides, it doesn't work like that. I could show them the portal, and they might not even be able to perceive it, let alone go through it. That's the way it works. That's what keeps my world safe from wholesale invasion. Most of the time, anyway. We do get retail now and then."

"In any event, it doesn't matter." She let out a breath. "I might as well tell you. I've been dropping nuclear grenades, a few dozen of them."

"Oh? Charming. Time-fused, I suppose, to go off . . . When, exactly?"

She checked a digital readout on the left sleeve of the suit.

"We have very little time."

ALECTO WHARF

SHE WAS A LITTLE SCHOONER, two-masted, patched sails and all, bulky and awkward as the worst of them. She didn't sail well to windward, he was told. Best to wait for a beam or following wind; but the wind didn't ordinarily oblige in the environs of Port of Dreams. He wouldn't wait, being too eager to get under way. He'd take her out on the tide.

The sky was dark, as it always was. But in the "morning hours" there was sometimes a sense that the dark roof had lifted. This was such a morning. The first morning of his eternity.

He stood astride the foredeck. He was the skipper. He even had a crew, four deckhands to pull the jib sheets and lash the boom and do the complete nautical thing.

"Do the complete nautical thing," he commanded.

"Aye, aye, sir." The one in front saluted with two fingers and turned to the crew.

"You heard 'im!"

They fanned out to do their various appointed tasks. They busied themselves with jib tack, mainsail lashing, shrouds and gaff jaws; with jib hanks and jib halyard and mainsail halyard; with burgee, peak, sail battens and pockets; with leech boom mainsheet and lifting rudder; tiller, extension, fairlead, and jib sheets; daggerboard, thwart, gooseneck, and tack; kicking strap, luff, mooring cleats, and pushpit.

"Bend on the sails!"

"Clip jib hanks on the forestay!"

"Attach the halyards!"

"Hoist the mainsail!"

"Tighten the boom vang!"

"The boomerang?"

"No, you pinhead. The boom vang!"

"Oh."

He watched appreciatively. They were a good crew. They were his crew. They were charging him a mint.

But they were worth it (they had told him). Boom vangs aside, they knew their mooring cleats from their cockpits, their foresail winches from their backstays, their steering compasses from their halyard winch and cleats. And, boy, did they know from tack downhaul, kicking strap, mainsheet, clew outhaul, topping lift, boom, tack, reefing points, leech, spreader, foresail hanks, shrouds, inner forestay, stanchion, toe rail, and fin keel!* These guys, like, *knew* all that stuff. . . .

A wind was rising, and the rivers flowed. . . .

(There was more than one river emptying into the Bay of Desires; in fact, the Bay was the confluence of no less than six rivers, making it the biggest fresh-water estuary in the afterworld. Rather, in this particular afterworld.)

The waters of the bay churned and boiled. The land fell away behind them. The roof of the sky lifted to a milky

---

*The author has obviously skimmed a few books on nautical lore and just as obviously does not know what any of these terms mean.

crepuscular darkness. Choppy waves thumped against the hull, and freshwater spray blessed their faces. They sailed on a close reach to the wind.

"We're under way, sir!"

"I noticed. Course, due west. Into the sun. Which there isn't."

"I noticed, sir."

"I'll brook no impertinence!"

"Sorry, sir."

"Or it's the crow's nest for you, swab."

"Sir, we have no crow's nest. This is a yacht, more or less."

"Well, see that you keep a respectful tongue in your head, or I'll clap you in irons and throw you in the brig."

"We have no brig, sir."

"Oh, shut up. Get below and brew me some coffee."

The shipyards boasted all manner of sailing craft. Many were of ancient design. There were barks and barges, galleys and longboats; but he had preferred a classic vessel from the zenith of the epoch of sail—humble as she was an example.

"Gods! I need a name for this ship."

He'd quite forgotten.

"The *Perilous* will be her name," he announced to the crew.

He had no idea why he'd chosen it.

"Good name, sir. Uh . . . though not exactly felicitous. Sailors are a suspicious lot. Could be trouble with the crew."

"Screw 'em if they can't take a joke."

"Aye, sir. Sir, did you get up on the wrong side of the hammock this morning?"

"Something's wrong with this whole deal. It's wearing thin."

"What's wearing thin, sir?"

"This afterlife. It's silly. For another thing, I don't belong here."

"You don't, sir? Where do you belong?"

"In another universe. This one . . . well, it—"

"It sucks, sir. Yes, many of the departed say that."

"You agree?"

"Well, sir, it's just a job to me. I'm not mortal, so I really don't know what death is. I should think it'd be a bit of nasty business, sir. Not pleasant, I assume."

"It could suck a bowling ball through fifty feet of garden hose."

"Striking image, sir."

"Thank you. But something tells me that I just don't belong in this cosmos. Something's wrong. Something's out of whack."

"Couldn't help you, sir."

"No, I guess you couldn't. Where's that coffee, by the way?"

"Steward's coming with it, sir."

"I smell salt!"

"There she lies, sir, dead ahead. The open sea."

"The Sea of Oblivion!"

The skipper took deep gulps of salt air. Above, a lone gull circled.

Or was it an albatross?

"What's out there?"

"We'll soon find out, sir."

"*I cannot rest from travel; I will drink life to the lees.*"

"This isn't life, sir."

"Be quiet for a minute. *All times I have enjoyed greatly, have suffered greatly, both with those that loved me, and alone; on shore, and when through scudding drifts the rainy Hyades vexed the dim sea.*"

"Nicely put, sir."

"Thanks. I read it in a fortune cookie."

"Do tell."

"Where's that damned coffee, Telemachus?"

"Here it is, sir!"

The steward gave him a steaming cup. He took it and drank. It burned his tongue gratifyingly.

*"And may there be no moaning of the bar when I put out to sea."**

Clouds gathered, blotting out the lightening sky. Darkness hovered. They sailed past the last spit of sand that stood between the estuary and the sea. The great foaming waters wailed against it in the darkness.

"So much for the no-moaning thing."

"Don't take too much stock in omens, sir."

"Right."

The *Perilous* sailed on into deepest night.

---

*From a poem by Geraldo Rivera. The quotation preceding is from a poem by Burt Reynolds.

Malnovia

THE SIGN above the door was in strange script but he knew
it read:

UNITED BROTHERHOOD OF MAGICIANS—
LOCAL 218

There was no handle on the door. No knocker either. The
door was starkly imposing, painted a shiny black.

Trent ran his hand over the surface. Smooth, very
smooth. And vibrating. The tension was incredible.

He backed away from the entrance and surveyed the front
of the building. It was undistinguished, slate-roofed and
sheathed in rough stone. A cozy little building of three
stories and a garret. Quaint dormers with peaked gables.
Very sedate.

He approached the door again and knocked once. There
came the suggestion of a vast, echoing interior.

"Okay," Trent said.

He stepped back again, looked the place up and down a
second time.

Then, suddenly, he spun once around, cape billowing, arms raised, and went into a dramatic stance, a configuration of power that conducted energy down from the ether, through his arms and into his hands. Power flowed out the ends of his fingers and shot straight at the shiny black barrier of the door.

The door flew open with a bang.

"Right."

Trent noticed that several people had stopped along the street to stare. He smiled, waved. They all hurried away.

He shrugged, then turned to regard the interior. It was dim. He walked to the door and looked in. A narrow corridor went off to the left an oddly long distance before it made an L. There was only the left turn, one way to go. He glanced outside and compared the dimensions of the building to the apparent length of the corridor. There was a disorienting mismatch.

"Neat trick."

He entered and began walking along the dark corridor toward the corner. He had gone only a half-dozen steps before the door slammed violently, shutting out all light and sound from the outside world.

All light, except that from his butane lighter, already out and burning. He held it high and proceeded with some caution, peering around the corner before turning it. The walk to the next L was even longer, and as he went along he heard strange noises up ahead. Sub-audial rumblings mixed with sharp, high-pitched squeaks, like a high-end stereo system with bowel trouble.

Then, more sounds. Subhuman growling. Groans. The scrabbling of claws. A scream.

He kept walking, whistling a nameless tune.

A bone-chilling demonic howl made him stop.

"Good, good." He smiled and nodded in admiration.

Another turn, and another. Leading nowhere.

He walked the maze for the next five minutes and got no nearer his goal, which, to his chagrin, was now a bathroom. He berated himself for not doing his business before entering. But a little nervousness can work its influence very quickly. And this, for all its mumbo jumbo, was nervous-making.

The butane lighter was getting hot. He snapped it off, and stood in darkness for a while.

When he clicked it on again the flame picked out the form of a monstrous creature, green-eyed and fearsomely clawed, advancing toward him out of the gloom.

"Hello there!" Trent greeted it. "Know where I can take a pee?"

"In your breeches, mortal," the demon roared, the chitin of its face splitting into a feculent smile.

"Ooops," Trent said.

Just before the flame went out, the demon lunged.

Darkness.

There came a hideous yowl; then, a burst of flame lit up the corridor. The flash diminished, subsided.

The remnants of something torn into several pieces lay smoking and burning on the floor.

Trent walked out of the shadows and bent to examine the remains, turning up his nose at the stench. He straightened up and stepped over them, walked on.

"Okay, people. I've seen the floor show. Now, when do I get some service?"

More screeching and howling came from up ahead.

"Right. I'm starting to get just a little annoyed."

The floor heaved and vibrated. The rough-boarded walls shook.

"Just a little ticked off, people."

Abruptly, everything ceased: the thunder, the shaking,

the horror-movie soundtrack. There was a doorway ahead, light coming through. He walked toward it.

He stepped out into a cramped office of crowded shelves, messy desks, gooseneck lamps, and general shabbiness. A closed door marked PRIVATE was set into the far wall.

There were two people in the room. A woman worked at a desk in the corner, hitting the keys of a curious machine that must have been a typewriter but looked like a medieval version of one. A man, short, stooped, and bespectacled—a real Bob Crachitt type, ink-sleeves and all—sat at a roll-top desk nearer the door, writing in a ledger with a long black pen, the point of which he dipped frequently into an squat ink bottle.

The woman, middle-aged and matronly in a bun and bifocals, kept typing, but the man looked up. He had thinning hair and a sallow face and smiled with large yellow teeth.

"What can I do for you, sir?"

Trent pocketed the Bic lighter.

"What was all that mummery about?"

The clerk's smile broadened. "Our apprentice test. You passed. Do you want to join the guild?"

"How much are dues?"

"A tithe of your yearly earnings. One third payable on signing a membership agreement, the second third due—"

"Not interested," Trent said. "I want information."

"Oh? How may I help you, sir?"

"I want to know who murdered my brother."

The clerk raised his bushy eyebrows. "Oh." He carefully laid down the pen. "I see. And your brother was . . . ?"

"Oh, come on."

"But I assure you, sir—"

"I want to see your boss. Who's the head honcho in this chickenshit outfit?"

"I beg your pardon? Sir, this is the office of the Chief Steward of Local 218. But I am afraid that at the moment, sir, he is not available. If you wish to make an appointment, I can do that for you."

"In about two minutes, I'm going to start taking this place apart beam from rafter."

"Sir, threats will not—"

Trent raised his arms and the room began to tremble.

"I can do the scary bits, too, you know."

The clerk looked around nervously.

The vibrations increased. Books fell from shelves, and a lamp toppled over. Ink sloshed over the clerk's ledger.

"Oh, dear!"

The woman shrieked and jumped up, hands clapped over her ears.

A section of ceiling plaster shattered on the clerk's already disorganized desk.

The clerk sprang to his feet and scurried toward the door marked PRIVATE.

"I'll see if the Steward will receive you!"

"Hey, thanks! Nice of you."

The clerk knocked first before he opened the door a crack and edged through.

"Nice day," Trent told the woman.

"Very nice," she said, nodding. She sat back down, fanned herself briefly with a file folder, then resumed pecking away at the anomalous typewriter.

Presently the clerk poked his head out.

"The Steward will see you."

"Oh? Well, that's kind of him, I must say. Thank you. Thank you very much."

The clerk ushered Trent in and slinked out, closing the door.

Trent surveyed the office into which he had stepped. It

was in sharp contrast to the anteroom. The carpeting was
thick enough to hide grazing sheep. The room was com-
fortably furnished in leathers, the walls covered in damask.
A marble fireplace stood to one side, burning cheerily.
Various objets d'art supplied accents around the room:
vases, statuary, decorated glass, a painting here and there.

The man at the desk had a long beard and wore a
traditional conical cap with stars and crescent moons. He
rose in greeting.

"Welcome, Trent, brother of Incarnadine."

"Hello. I have the honor of addressing—?"

"Mylor, at your service, my lord."

"I hope I am not disturbing you?"

"Not at all. Please sit down. May I offer you refresh-
ment?"

"None, thank you."

"Please, my lord, make yourself comfortable."

Trent took his seat in one of the wing chairs by the
fireplace. Mylor came round the desk and took the one
opposite.

"How may I serve you, prince of Perilous?"

"Ah, so you know our home world?"

"Well. I've visited Castle Perilous on occasion. I was on
good terms with your distinguished brother. A fine man. A
great magician. One of the greatest, possibly, in the entire
cosmos."

"Yet someone here killed him."

Mylor stared into the flames before saying, "You're quite
sure of that?"

"Yes. I recognize the hand at work. At least, I think I do.
It could be one of a number of people, actually. But I do
know this for sure. Somebody from Perilous is here and is
working magic, possibly in conjunction with one of your
people."

Mylor continued to find something of interest in the flickering firelight.

After a long interval he stated, "This is very disturbing indeed."

"All I ask of you is to tell me if there is someone from Perilous here. And if so, where is he?"

"My lord, you place me in an awkward situation."

"No doubt."

"On the one hand, I wish to see justice done. On the other, in my capacity as an official of the Guild I cannot betray a fellow member. If there has been wrongdoing, the matter must be handled by the Guild itself. I cannot in good conscience permit outside interference."

"I understand," Trent said. "But you must understand my position. I must bring my brother's murderer to justice or my chance at the throne is in jeopardy."

"I did not know you were the heir apparent."

"There is some contention over that point. And now the shadow of suspicion falls on me concerning my brother's death."

"Naturally. Still, my lord, there is not much I can do save look into the matter myself with a view toward a possible internal investigation."

"Pardon me for saying so, but I don't trust the Guild to dispense justice. You guys run a cozy little club here. You look out for your own. My brother was doubtless viewed as an intruder here in this world—"

"He was a Guild member."

"Naturally, Inky wouldn't scab. But he was probably resented. After all, he was Court Magician to the Elector. A juicy little plum of a post."

"And was soon to be appointed to the court of His Imperial Majesty."

"Ah-hah." Trent nodded appreciatively. "Thank you.

Thank you very much for that. But I suppose you couldn't tell me who else was in line for the job."

"That I'm afraid I couldn't do, no."

"I see. Well, now I know the motive. It seems to me that a spell that could kill Inky would be a major one. I don't quite understand how it could have overcome Inky's defenses or how anyone here could have whipped up a spell that powerful. But it worked, so I have to assume it was a real lulu."

"It still is."

"Eh? You mean it's still working?"

"Yes. It's been giving me headaches for days. And my teeth hurt."

"Still working," Trent repeated with a puzzled frown. "I don't get it."

"Neither do I."

"You know the source."

"Naturally."

"But you won't reveal it."

"I am constrained by many things, not the least of which is the penalty I would incur by violating my oath of membership in the Guild."

"I quite understand. But can you tell me this? Does this big spell have transuniversal dimensions?"

"I suspect so. Otherwise I don't understand the need for all the power. It's been draining reserves around here."

"And it's still working. That's a riddle, that is."

"Perplexing. As I said, it's putting a considerable strain on the local dynamics. I'd be most pleased if the spell were to cease operation."

"Let me see if something can't be done about that."

"You'll be going up against one of the best locals. He's pretty good. And teamed up with your compatriot, he might be invincible."

"You're forgetting one thing," Trent said. "The spell's taking all his power."

"Why, yes, of course. You're absolutely right. Unless they can disengage it temporarily."

"I've a hunch they can't."

"Let's hope you're right about that, too."

"One more thing. If I can identify the vibrations, I can locate the source. But I'm not familiar enough with the local harmonics. Does your oath forbid coaching me?"

"Not at all. Though it might be difficult to do."

"Can you give me a musical analogue?"

"That's all you'd need?"

"I think."

"Fine, but I don't know your musical system."

"You know the one Inky was fond of?"

"Oh. Yes, it's similar to ours. Let's see if I can . . ." Mylor thought a moment.

"The spell's carrier vibrations are tuned to the key of C-sharp minor, with modulations to A minor and F minor."

"So that was what all that background spookiness I noticed on arrival here was? Thought it was just the magical din of the city. *That's* the spell?"

"That's it. Is that sufficient for you? You have perfect pitch, I take it."

"Yes, a family trait." Trent smiled. "You've been most helpful."

"And I think I did it without risk of waking up someday with my body parts artfully positioned around the room."

"You didn't have to, but you did."

Mylor smiled back. "I didn't want you taking this place apart beam from rafter."

Trent chuckled. "Sorry about that. Didn't know what I was up against."

"Sorry I didn't recognize you right off. Should have."

" 'Tis nothing. Well, I shall be leaving."

They rose and shook hands.

"Good luck," Mylor said. "Of course, I'll be starting an official investigation, the wheels of which will no doubt turn much too slowly for your satisfaction."

"You're right. But all I need is some proof, proof to take back and confront the Privy Council with. Or least firm knowledge of who the culprit was. I'll try not to muddy the waters too much here. I just want my guy. Your guy I'll leave to you."

"I appreciate that."

"And thanks again."

"Don't mention it."

Mylor showed his guest out.

Passing the clerk's desk, Trent dropped a gold coin into the mess of paperwork.

"Bob, take the rest of the day off. And a Merry Christmas to you."

"Why, thank you, s—"

Bob did a take. "I beg your pardon?"

Trent stepped through the outer door into a long waiting room. Gone was the maze. A man and a woman were waiting, reading magazines. They looked up as he passed through.

"They let witches into the Guild?" Trent asked of her.

She was quite pretty.

"Not all female magicians are witches," she said pleasantly.

"They badgered us until we had to let them in," the man complained.

"Albin, how would you like spending the rest of the day sunning yourself on a lily pad out in the goldfish pond?"

"Ree-deeep," Albin said sheepishly and hid his face in the dogeared pages of *Occult Weekly*.

Laughing, Trent went out the door.

MINE

RUNNING IN THE DARK, running from sounds of pursuit. Turning corners into blind alleys. Running, always running, desperately looking for another safety shaft, a way up, a way out.

Running and running some more.

Past arsenals of the tools of war, high-tech weapon in hand, racing through darkness, pounding footsteps echoed by those at your back, drawing, it seems, ever nearer. Gaining. Endless dark tunnel ahead.

Gene stopped to peer around a corner. Nothing coming, so he waved Sativa on. She ran past him, turned the corner, and sprinted ten yards before ducking behind a pile of shipping containers. He came out from cover, dashed past her position and took a firing position between two refrigerator-size plastic crates. He watched Sativa advance down the tunnel at a crouching lope.

In this manner they kept moving through the underground warren, dodging unseen pursuers whose voices sometimes rose to a shout.

But it was not long before pursued met pursuer.

Gene turned the corner and surprised a man in combat fatigues and futuristic helmet bolting out of an ambush position, apparently unaware of Gene's approach. Gene fired wildly, two shots, and ducked for cover.

The gun made a curious sound, rather like a crossbow, perhaps louder. But it was nothing like the ear-splitting crack of a conventional weapon.

He heard a groan and looked over the edge of the crate. The man was lying supine, his weapon out of reach.

Gene rose from cover as Sativa came jogging past. She went to the man and leaned over him.

The rebel solider turned his head and scanned her through red night-sight goggles.

She raised her weapon and aimed at his chest.

"Sativa, no!"

Gene's shout was in vain. She fired, and the man died as Gene looked helplessly on.

She met his bewildered look with a face twisted by hatred and the immense effort of self-justification.

"You don't understand. Members of my family have died in their terrorist attacks. My half-brother was tortured to death by these scum."

He said nothing.

"Let's try this direction. I don't think—"

Shouts in the direction in which she pointed drove them back, but that route also had its disadvantages. More voices and more boots thumping against the level tunnel floor.

Fairly soon, no direction seemed likely to yield an escape route. Shots came out of the darkness at them.

They took up positions on opposite sides of the tunnel and alternated fire in both directions.

Gene wondered how many rounds his weapon had, trying

to remember whether she had told him seven hundred or seventeen hundred—or was it just seventy?

He sprayed on full automatic for a while, then switched to single shot in case the lowest figure was correct. He had two extra clips in his knapsack but doubted he could reload under fire. It had been difficult enough in "training."

Slugs chunked into the wall near him, not ricocheting even when hitting at a sharp angle. They packed a lot of wallop, these weapons did. The man Sativa had shot would probably have died in any case, possibly from shock alone. With that grim consolation, Gene assuaged his feeling of half-earned guilt.

But that wasn't really bothering him. The prospect of imminent death was. They were trapped, and this was possibly the end. As he fired, he thought of giving up.

No. There had been a death; an execution, yet. As he saw it, that pretty much blew chances for a negotiated settlement or clemency on the captors' part. Anyway, Sativa probably had not lied about these guys. They certainly weren't pulling any punches.

Or were they? They were returning fire very conservatively.

Of course. They were afraid of setting off all this ammo.

Sativa wasn't. She had turned into a human Gatling gun, spitting death in both directions.

How much longer before the nuke grenades went off?

Nuclear grenades. Really, now. He couldn't conceive of it. It seemed like a joke. . . .

He watched in amazement as Sativa threw something in one direction, hauled back, and heaved something in the other.

Nuke grenades in the tunnel?

"Concussion squibs! Get down!"

Gene hunkered down just in time. Twin flashes dazzled

him, and two bone-shaking concussions jarred him one way, then the other. He wound up on his buttocks, wedged in tight.

She yanked him out and pushed him forward.

"Get, get!"

He got, running through thin smoke and jumping over still bodies.

"*Cottleston, Cottleston, Cottleston pie!*" he yelled as he brought the butt of his rifle around to connect with an enemy face mask. He ran on into the darkness, virtually blind.

He collided with someone, rolled, and bounced to his feet again, racing on. He cracked his hip against something, almost tripped again, dimly saw a corner to turn and turned it.

A half-minute later he was still sprinting through total darkness, somehow using his magical sensors, when he heard Sativa's hoarse shout behind him.

He sensed something up ahead, a barrier. He slowed to avoid banging up against the gigantic metal door that blocked the end of the tunnel.

She came running up, bringing her ghostly glow with her.

"You've found it!"

"What? Oh, the freight entrance."

"Yes!" She dragged him backwards. "We've got to arm the launcher."

"Right."

He followed her back down the tunnel to the nearest intersection. When they got there, shots drove them back.

"Give it to me!"

He took the launcher off his back and handed it over.

"Cover!"

He took up a position at the corner and began concentrating fire on the tunnel segment to the right. Answering fire was more responsive here, as the tunnel was less cluttered with munitions in this area. He switched his weapon back to automatic and hosed in both directions to keep enemy heads and weapons down.

Sativa worked furiously behind his back. But soon she was ready. Balancing the firing tube on her shoulder, she took aim at the blind end of the tunnel.

"Get down and cover your eyes!"

"We're too close!"

"Move!"

He stretched out and tried to make himself one with the wall, burying his face in his shirt-sleeve.

"You're right, this ought to kill us," she said almost casually a second before he squeezed the trigger.

The missile left the tube with an ear-splitting *whoosh* of flame.

A split second before the world came apart he felt her weight on his back, felt her shielding him with her body.

More light than he'd ever suspected to exist turned the mine into the interior of a star.

He couldn't get up at first. She was lying on his legs; he pushed her off and struggled to his feet. He bent to pick her up, couldn't quite. He slapped her face a few times.

He did manage to drag her a few feet before she woke up.

"I can walk," she yelled.

He helped her up and she could walk a bit. There was light coming from the blasted end of the tunnel, which was now a gaping hole in the side of the mountain. Together, they staggered toward blinding day.

Just as they came out into the world she lurched and fell. He lost his grip on her and she rolled down the crumbling slope of the mountain. He ran after her, fell, and rolled until he was brought up against her still form.

There was a gaping hole in her chest, blood fountaining out.

"Run," she said. "The grenades . . . chain explosion . . ." A spasm went through her body.

She died in the interval between heartbeats.

He made his way down the mountain—running, stumbling, falling, sometimes all three at once. He slid the remainder of the way and ended up half-buried in a pile of mine tailings.

He got up and ran, amazed that he was essentially unhurt, no bones broken. His hands were scratched but that was the extent of the damage.

He began to sprint, wondering how far you'd have to run to be safe from multiple nuclear blasts—and possible chain-reaction secondary explosions. Pretty far, he guessed.

He ran across bare desert floor and jumped a narrow dry wash. When he came to another, this one wider and deeper, he dove in and took cover.

About fifteen seconds later the mountain went up. But it was a surprisingly muffled, subdued affair. Smoke issued from the ventilation shafts along the peak of the mountain, then flames reared up. A tongue of fire licked out from the tunnel mouth, then turned to black smoke. A few seconds later a series of smaller explosions began and continued for the next several minutes. The mine turned into a nuclear inferno.

By that time he had begun to walk home.

He came trudging through the portal, stepping from that too-colorful world of blue and yellow rocks into the relative drabness of the castle.

He felt a slight jar as he passed through, a signal that there was some time displacement. Every universe has its own clock, its own rate of time flow. Spend an hour in a different world and a day might go by in the universe you left. Gene had developed a sixth sense about it; he could usually guess how much time had passed in the castle since his departure.

It felt like half a week, castle time, give or take a day. He'd only been gone, at most, six hours in subjective time. He wondered what had happened, if anything, in his absence. Probably nothing.

He came into the sitting room and collapsed on the settee. He wasn't hurt. He had defied death again. He wondered why he liked to do that.

Silly. Very silly to keep doing it. One of these times he was going to be just a tad too silly and get his ticket punched.

He thought about Sativa.

Then he decided not to think about Sativa. Sativa belonged in another world. Her world was not his. No need to think of her at all. She wasn't part of reality.

He thought about her anyway. He thought of her face and how pretty it was. Then the face became distorted by hate.

He didn't want to think about her. He didn't want to do anything just now except rest. He'd go to his room, catch a shower, and go to bed. When he got up he'd eat, then maybe go to the Gaming Hall and see what was cooking there. Maybe somebody wanted to get up a few rubbers of bridge. Or cribbage. Or whist or something. Trivial Pursuit?

He saw purple eyes and white hair.

Funny, it didn't look *old* white, like hair on an old person. It was just white. Like the whitest blond. A little whiter than corn silk.

But she didn't exist any longer. Her world—her worlds—didn't really exist. Nothing really existed but the castle.

The places on the other side of these portals weren't real,

he told himself. They were movies. Yeah. They were 3-D Technicolor movies in Cinerama and Panavision with Dolby stereo sound. You could walk through them.

She'd been nothing but celluloid, the kind of stuff that dreams are made on. . . .

Dreams.

SEASIDE

DREAMS.

She'd had a doozy last night. Crazy stuff.

Linda poured another cup of coffee, added a dab of milk. No sugar, and she hated the substitute. She drank and looked out her kitchen window with its view of palm trees, Santa Monica beach, and the wide Pacific. The moon was still up, setting in the west.

> *Then felt I like some watcher of the skies*
> *When a new planet swims into his ken;*
> *Or like stout Cortez when with eagle eyes*
> *He star'd at the Pacific—and all his men*
> *Look'd at each other with a wild surmise—*
> *Silent, upon a peak in Darien.**

Crazy dream about a castle.

The phone rang and she reached for it.

"Hello?"

---

*Yet another snippet of verse by a TV personality, this one from Oprah Winfrey.

"Hi! Up early, are you?"

"Hello, John, dearest. I had a nutty dream about you last night."

"Oh? Sexy, I hope."

"Well, sort of. You were a king in a magic castle."

"Great. What were you?"

"A witch, I think. I could do magic. So could you. And then . . . it got scary."

"What, the dream?"

"Yeah. I don't want to talk about it. Something happened to you, and I woke up in a sweat."

"You okay?"

"Sure. It was just a dream. Listen, do you want to do lunch today?"

"Why not? And dinner. And more."

She smiled. "I like the 'more' part. I love you."

"I love you, Linda."

"Are we still on for the trip up to Tahoe?"

"You bet. We leave Friday night."

"It'll be nice. I'm glad I met you, John."

"Been nice so far, hasn't it? Me, a king? You know, that doesn't sound so bad."

"It was strange—the dream, I mean. It was so *involved*. Did you ever have a dream that seemed so real and so detailed that you think, Where am I getting this stuff?"

"All the time. I dream all the time, Linda. In fact, last night I dreamed that I died."

"Oh, how awful. Are *you* okay?"

"Sure. But how can we tell when we're dreaming, Linda? Maybe this is a dream."

"I'm getting such a weird feeling hearing you say that."

She looked out the window. Palm trees, bright sun, the bright blue Pacific. Didn't she belong here? What could be wrong? What could possibly be . . . ?

"John? Hello?"

The phone had gone dead.

And now night was falling. The sun sank into the darkening ocean. The moon fell out of the sky and the stars threw down their spears. . . .

"No!"

She dropped the phone and screamed.

She awoke screaming.

The room came into focus. Her room, her suite in the Guest Residence, at Castle Perilous.

Arms wrapped about herself, legs crossed, she sat on the bed and trembled for several minutes. Then she got up and went to the bathroom.

When she came out she poured herself a drink of water from the pitcher on the night table. She gulped it down.

She collapsed back onto the bed and pulled the covers up snugly around her.

And fell back into dream.

SEA OF OBLIVION

THE NIGHT WIND BLEW with steady force. The crew hoisted
the spinnaker and the big sail bloomed proudly off the
bow.

The albatross followed, circling in the darkness, a white
form like a ghost in the night.

"I don't like the looks of that bird," he allowed.

"Tekeli-li!" came the call of the albatross.

Apart from that, he was still enjoying doing the skipper
thing: shouting orders, bellowing his displeasure, slurping
coffee, spitting it over the side and complaining.

"Bilge water! Brew me up something potable!"

"Aye, Cap'n! You'd like, maybe cappuccino?"

"Just espresso."

"How about a pastry to go with that, sir?"

"You have cannoli?"

"Plain or chocolate?"

"By 'plain' I hope you mean vanilla."

"Yes, sir, I mean vanilla, sir."

"With the dark chocolate chips, right?"

"Yes, sir!"

"Just the chips, none of the candied fruit nonsense."

"Sir, I would say that these are your purist's cannoli, sir."

"Fine, bring me one. After dinner."

"What will you be eating for dinner, sir?"

"What d'you have?"

"Milk-fed veal, sir."

"Well, wring some out and bring me a glass."

"That's not very original, sir."

"I'm still waiting for that coffee, Telly! The longer I wait, the fouler the weather to come!"

"Aye, aye, sir!"

Telly left the bridge and the skipper to his thoughts.

He had none. He couldn't think, he could only go through this dumb show, this pretense, this playacting . . . this—?

Yes, what the hell was it? Where was he? Why couldn't he remember anything? He was tired of all this.

Perhaps he *was* starting to remember.

He scanned the sky. That remark about bad weather had been prescient. He saw flashes, then heard far-off thunder.

"Storm off the starboard beam!"

"Tekeli-li!" the albatross cried.

The storm-blast came and whipped the sea to a frenzy. Whitecaps rose like ice-cream cones and white foam curdled and clotted across the face of the deep. The ship rocked in its cradle of the ocean. Mist gathered and snow fell, and it grew wondrous cold. Icebergs, mast-high, floated by.

Saint Elmo's fire blazed on the masthead and about the rigging.

"Nice touch."

"Coffee, sir!"

He took the coffee. "Well, it's about time. Pretty storm, eh? What's it all about, Telly?"

"What are storms usually about, skipper?"

"Oh, I dunno. About nature, the elements. Life. About man and woman, birth, death and infinity. And like that. Did you put Sweet 'N Low in this?"

"Sir, our sugar stores are way down."

"We just put out!"

"Sorry, everything's wet down in the galley. We're shipping water."

"Well, next time send it Federal Express. God, this is awful. I hate diet soda, too. Leaves an aftertaste. Know what I mean?"

"I do, sir, but I have a weight problem."

"Are you kidding? Why you're as svelte as a mackerel. Look at this gut."

"Tekeli-li!" the albatross screamed as it wheeled in the stormy sky.

"I wish that frigging bird would shut up."

"It's an omen, sir."

"Omen of what?"

"Can be a good omen, sir; can be a bad omen."

"Well, what species is that critter?"

"I'd say pretty bad, sir."

"Tekeli-li!"

"I'll give you 'Tekeli-li,' you mangy bird. Telly, fetch my Hawken .50 caliber from the ordnance locker."

"Sir, but—!"

"No buts. *Tout de suite.*"

Telemachus fetched it *tout de suite.*

"Hey, he's gonna shoot the albatross!"

Telly's announcement was met by wailing and moaning among the crew.

"Forbear, Cap'n! Don't do it!"

"Oh, why not," the skipper chided. "It's just a damned bit of wildfowl."

"I fear thee, Ancient Mariner!"

He took aim and fired. A puff of feathers bloomed in the dark sky.

Presently, something thudded against the deck. And there it lay on the glistening boards, still and bloodied.

"That's no albatross! You! What's-your-name!"

"Morry, sir."

"Morry, take a look at that thing."

"I'm looking at it, sir."

"What is it?"

"It's a chicken."

"A goddamned *chicken*?"

"Yes, sir."

He turned to Telly. "So, what the hell is this?"

"I don't know, sir. You shouldn't have shot it."

"What the hell's a chicken doing out here?"

"Er . . . chicken of the sea?"

He raised the rifle. "That's two."

Telly ran from the bridge.

The skipper noticed that the ship had grown a bit bigger; it was now, in fact, a three-masted schooner.

"Or perhaps a salmon packet," he mused.*

Anyway, the *Perilous* was now a full-fledged sailing vessel, and he speculated that this transformation was meant to appease him in some way. Perhaps his complaints had been heard.

Didn't make a damn bit of difference. He was fairly sure he didn't want any part of this.

The wind blew out of the clouds, and the clouds— noctilucent, almost ectoplasmic—raced by like spirits. Rain pelted the deck and beat against the sails while the wind whipped them about.

---

*Your guess is as good as mine.

"And I'm really getting tired of the footnotes, too!" he shouted.*

The storm was putting on quite a show. Too good a show, in fact. The ship bobbed liked a cork.

He lashed himself to the helm. Then he lashed himself to the mast. When none of that worked, he lashed Telly.

"Hey, what the hell are you lashing me for, Cap'n?"

"You're handy."

"Put down that lash!"

"Sorry I flared. Look, this has got to stop."

"What's got to stop?"

"This sham, this entire bamboozle."

"Are you insinuating that this is all some sort of put-on?"

"That is exactly what I am insinuating. Look."

He raised his hands against the storm.

In an instant, the sea calmed, the wind subsided, and part of the backdrop fell over to reveal a brick wall.

"See?"

"Aw, you're no fun."

"Now, what kind of afterlife d'you call that?"

Telly raised his hands apologetically. "It's the best we can do."

"Well, it's not good enough. I'm jumping ship."

"What? You can't do that."

"Why not? I refuse to go through with this nonsense."

"But, you must. You're dead, and you have to have an afterlife."

"I may be dead, but I'll be damned if I'll have an afterlife. I mean, what's the point? Is there an afterlife after the afterlife?"

---

*This is a self-referential textual allusion, a device much favored by "postmodernist" writers. This is by far the cleverest touch in the book; but it is by no means original.

"No."

"Why not? Seems to me you could just go on and on. Pointless. Why not let it end? Give it a rest. When it's over it's over."

"But you don't understand."

"Oh, I think I do. By the way, I remember my name."

"Oh, that's nice. What is it?"

"I'm Ed McMahon. You may already be a winner."*

"Seriously . . ."

"I'm serious! I'm checking out."

"You can't."

"I'm cashing in my chips. I'm vacating the premises. I'm history. I am one with Nineveh and Tyre."

"I take it you mean this."

He went to the rail, climbed up on it and stood regarding the "deep." It was more or less a swimming pool backed by a lighted cyclorama, as in a TV or film studio.

"I don't even believe this," he said, scowling.

The studio, too, faded away. All that was left was the ship, adrift in a gray void, an indeterminate nothingness.

"Telemachus" was still there. He said, "You'll drift alone, forever, through eternity."

"Better that than this charade."

"You might change your mind," came the warning. "But then it will be too late, Ed."

"Let me worry about that. By the way, my name is Incarnadine."

He jumped from the rail.

And fell . . . and fell . . . and fell . . .

---

*If Ed McMahon has written any poetry, it is to date unpublished, although rumors abound that there exists a holograph manuscript of something called The "Heerrrrre's Johnny!" Cantos. By the way, this is the last footnote. I'd like to extend a thank-you to the footnote staff for a job well done. Nice work, people.

MALNOVIA

THE HOUSE STOOD at the end of a cul-de-sac off a side street in the middle-class section of the city. It wasn't a bad house. Big oak beams alternated with off-white stucco, steep gables topping it all off. Otherwise undistinguished. It was a quiet little lane; a mews, really; an alley.

But it was definitely the source of the spookiness.

Trent stood at the corner and checked things out. This was a very tranquil location, tucked away from the bustle of the city yet right in the heart of things. Perfect neighborhood for a little *pied-à-terre*. For trysts. Afternoon assignations. A sordid affair or two.

He walked down the lane, checking each house as he passed. Discreet neighbors; keep to themselves. Never gossip. Oh, no.

Even a pleasant tree or two at the curb; beeches. Some shrubbery. Clean sidewalk. Very nice indeed.

He stopped in front of the pseudo-Tudor affair and stood arms akimbo, casing the joint. Rather narrow. Nice windows. Oops, one cracked, there. The place could use a coat of whitewash. Or maybe a warm earth-tone—buff, beige, whatever. Be daring—puce.

The door was one step up from the sidewalk. Again, coated with what looked like black lacquer. This one had a knob and a bronze knocker, though.

He tried the knocker and waited.

"Read your meter!" he called.

He tried the knob. It turned. The door opened.

"Well, now."

He went in and shut the door. Inside was a vestibule with a coat rack and a tall mirror. He passed through this and entered a hallway that continued past a stairway to a distant kitchen. The top of the stairs was dark. To the right lay the parlor, and this he decided to explore first.

The room was dark and stuffy, chock full of curios and bric-a-brac: stuffed birds; statuary of low-brow taste favoring the theme of mythical animals; horological charts and other posters featuring things astrological; a chart on the science of metoposcopy, showing the salient features of the human visage, especially the lines of the forehead; many incense burners—in fact the place was redolent of sandalwood—hundreds of decorative candles, many of them black; a number of pieces of primitive art, medicine masks and such; an ancient mummy case, standing in a corner; innumerable pentacles and mystical signs; decorated cups and chalices and bowls having a ceremonial look about them; more candles; more pentacles; more paraphernalia associated with a wide variety of occult disciplines: phrenology, cheiromancy, cartomancy, alchemy, and on and on.

The place reeked of magic. Cheap magic.

He rolled back a wooden door and walked into a dining area usurped by more quaint clutter.

The kitchen was a mess.

He came down the hall to the foot of the stairs and listened. Faint music.

As he mounted the staircase he recognized the piece: the "Moonlight" sonata, in C-sharp minor. Good spooky tune.

Something was coalescing at the top of the stairs. At least, something was trying to come together. He stopped to let it.

The thing finally materialized. Another demon, rather haphazardly formed. Botched around the legs. It was properly scaled and fanged, though, and looked fearsome enough.

Demon and human locked eyes for a moment.

The demon said, "You're violating private property."

"The real estate agent said to go right in."

"Oh . . . huh?"

"Actually, I'm selling Girl Scout cookies. You want S'mores?"

"Don't toy with me!"

The demon made swiping motions with sharp claws and snapped its crooked yellow teeth.

Trent observed, arms folded.

The demon presently ceased these blandishments. It stared vacantly.

Trent said loudly, "Well?"

The thing raised its arms in a gesture of exasperated hopelessness. "Oh, *shit*! Forget it! Forget I said anything! Excuse me, I'll just go back to my needlepoint."

It stalked off, grumbling its disgust. A door slammed.

Trent chuckled as he went up the steps.

There were three bedrooms. He didn't bother with the one the demon had entered. The one at the top of the stairs was stuffed with crates and boxes. That left the front bedroom.

This door was locked.

He tried a spell and got the lock unlocked all right, but he sensed a redundancy of chains and latches and deadbolts and such on the other side. Deciding to drop subtlety, he blew the son-of-a-bitching thing in with a moderate blast.

The door became a puff of sawdust mixed with plaster dust from sections of wall. When the dust settled, he walked in.

And there, in a room full of books, sitting at a large circular table, was a man in black robes and conical hat, playing solitaire. He was middle-aged with mutton-chop sideburns and thick black-framed glasses. He looked up with a cheery, confident smile, showing small feral teeth.

"Glad you could come. Prince Trent, I presume."

"The same," Trent answered. "What goes on here?"

The man chuckled. "You know, you *did* break into my house. I really should protest."

"Your front door was open. Now, this is an interesting device."

He referred to what lay in the middle of the table. It was an oblong block of some transparent substance—not glass; most likely Plexiglas. Embedded inside it was a miniature figure, a doll. The block had been positioned in the middle of a very primitive-looking pentacle carved into the wood of the circular table.

Trent bent to peer at the figure. It was a good likeness.

"What the heck is this?" Trent studied the patterns. "Don't tell me it's . . . voodoo?"

The man chuckled again. "You got it."

Trent straightened, pushed back his plumed hat and laughed. "Well, I'll be damned. You blind-sided Inky with a zombie spell?"

"Sometimes the simplest approach works best. I like primitive magic. It works well against sophisticates. As you said, 'blind-sided.' "

"You sucker-punched him."

The man laughed. "It worked."

"But—" Trent had to laugh, too. He began a tour of the room, reading book spines and examining curios. Mostly there were books; stuffed shelves reached to the ceiling and blanketed the walls. It wasn't a bad collection, mostly on the occult.

An old Victrola was scratchily playing the "Moonlight."

The man said, "By the way, the name is Ruthven."

"So, Ruthven," Trent said. "Let me guess. You do most of your business running the little con. F'rinstance, you hex a field of barley and then hoodwink the poor farmer into hiring you to ward off the evil spirits causing the blight."

"That one's older than dirt."

"Or put the kibosh on a tinker's business and sell him liability insurance, so to speak."

"Always a good one. You're right, the standard scams. I like to keep to basics. I make a fair living."

Trent gestured toward the table. "But this . . . *this*, for all its primitivism, is rather ambitious."

"Yeah." Ruthven played another card. "I want to retire soon. I don't have much money saved. I like the ladies, if you know what I mean. I like a good time. So I've been something less than prudent. Consequently, when someone at the castle came to me with a proposition, I jumped at the chance."

"Someone at the castle," Trent mused, still strolling.

As he passed by a closet he reached out and yanked the door open, and continued on.

"These are modern times, Tragg. Come out of the closet."

A timorous, worried Lord Tragg came out of his hiding place.

"It wasn't my idea!"

Ruthven chortled at that.

"No?" Trent kept on peering at book titles. "Whose, then?"

"This man!" Tragg pointed at his accomplice. "He came to me!"

"Give it up, Tragg," Ruthven said. "You're no actor."

Tragg sniffed. "Oh, I admit I wanted Incarnadine out of the way. Our enmity goes back centuries. He's done me no end of wrong. He cuckolded me, once, long ago. My first wife."

"Doesn't sound like Inky," Trent said. "But anyway, go on."

"Well, my wife and I weren't married at the time, but—"

"Then your terminology is a little skewed."

"But that was only one of the slights he paid me, a single instance of the wrongs that he has done me."

"I'm still listening."

"Why, he once sued my estate for back taxes that nearly ruined me!"

"And he probably never collected. He's too easy on tax dodgers and scofflaws. That's one of my beefs about Inky. But, continue, please."

"I won't recite the litany. Suffice it to say that I have ample and sufficient justification—"

"You have bupkis."

"I *beg* your pardon, sir. This coarse phraseology you tend to use is most indecorous. Really, sir!"

"Tragg, shut up."

Tragg did.

Trent circled back to the table. "So, Inky's not dead."

"He won't last long in a sealed sarcophagus," Ruthven told him. "Takes only half an hour or so. Even if he has air, he won't last long."

"Very slick. A sleeping spell. One that induces a sleep deep enough to pass for death."

"It does pass easily enough," Ruthven said. "There are signs to look for, tip-offs, but you have to know what they are. Most doctors would sign the death certificate without question."

"You fooled Mirabilis," Trent said. "And he's good."

"I knew it would work," Ruthven said. "But I wasn't sure how long it would last. With anyone else, I wouldn't have worried. But when you deal with a magician as powerful as your brother, there's every chance that he could break the spell and come out of the sleep. So I had the castle undertaker—one of Tragg's buddies—pretend he couldn't cast the preservation spell. Of course, this tipped you off—"

"WHAT!" Tragg was astounded. "You had Miron spill the beans? Of all the harebrained . . ."

"I *told* you," Ruthven said irritably. "His lying in state for ten days was way too risky. He would have come to and then our gooses would have been done to a turn. I had to shorten the whole process and that was the only way to do it."

"But, letting *him* find out. That's insane!"

"Is it?" Ruthven looked at Trent. "You know, Trent, this is redounding to your benefit. You're Regent because of me. I did for you what you once tried to do for yourself. And if you stick with me, I can make you King of Perilous. Permanent."

"Do away with Brandon."

"And nobody will know. Nobody. It's a good scam, Your Excellency. I'm willing to cut you in for a piece of the action."

Trent smiled. "What about your buddy Tragg, here?"

"Tragg's about as much good to me as mammaries on a satyr."

Tragg began to turn a distinct shade of magenta.

Ruthven went on, "I was going to approach you, but I didn't know you. You're royalty and you'd hardly have deigned to team up with the likes of me. So I used Tragg as a cat's-paw."

"And you figured that when I copped to this setup I'd throw in with you."

"That's the way I figured it. Did I figure right?"

"What's in it for you?"

"Like I said, I want to retire. I want to live in Perilous. Not the castle itself, or course. Drafty old barn. I want to be set up in my own world. A nice situation. A little palace, mostly women servants, hand-picked. You get the picture. Some comfort in my old age. Everything I've ever wanted."

"I see." Trent nodded slowly. "I see." He took a deep breath. "Ruthven, I'm afraid I'm going to have to disappoint you. No deal."

Tragg seemed relieved.

"Mind telling me why?" Ruthven asked as he went back to his game of solitaire.

"No, not at all. If you had asked me fifty, a hundred years ago, I might have taken you up on it. But things change, people change. I no longer want the throne."

Tragg was surprised. "But in Privy Council chambers you were adamant—"

"I've been at the job two days and I'm sure I don't want it. If I'd known long ago what the job entailed I would have given up all interest then. But I didn't. I probably never really was interested. It's probably some kind of psychological quirk and very likely has something to do with my relationship with my father. But all that is entirely beside the point. I'm not going to murder Inky."

"You really disappoint me, Trent," Ruthven said.

"You'll address me as 'Your Royal Highness.' "

"So, sorry. But you really do. Here I thought you were a smart guy."

"I am a smart guy. I'm also a lazy guy. I like boating, swimming, and making love on the beach at night. You can have castles and dungeons and the whole bit. Not my cup of tea."

"That's too bad. We could have made a great team."

"I'm not a team player, Ruthven."

"Like I said, too bad."

"So, I'm afraid your little project is over," Trent told him, reaching for the block of Plexiglas . . . or was it Lucite?

"Not so fast," Ruthven said. He had an enormous pistol in his hand. "I can't let you do that."

"You *must* not break the spell!" Tragg shouted.

"Why not?" Trent asked innocently, his hand poised above the curious artifact.

"If the spell is abrogated prematurely, the spirits we've evoked and compacted with will have leave to tear us to bits!"

"Sorry. That's hardly my worry."

Ruthven cocked the pistol. "I'm warning you. Hands off."

"Ruthven, you're not even a rat. You're a mouse going to rat night-school."

"Okay, my friend. You asked for it."

From the pistol there came a popping sound. Ruthven's eyes widened in utter astonishment as a rod extruded from the end of the barrel. From around it a square of cloth unfurled. On the cloth was lettering: BANG!!

"What the blazes—?"

Trent grabbed the transparent block. A loud snapping sound was heard.

Tragg gasped, "The spell!"

Trent examined the block. "It is Lucite, isn't it? You know, I ought to give this to Inky as a present next Solstice. He's a science-fiction writer. He ought to appreciate a totally worthless block of Lucite."*

---

*Sorry, one more thing. The publisher has requested clarification of this in-joke. The comment about the block of worthless Lucite is a clear dig at the annual Nebula Awards, given by the SFWA (the Science Fiction Writers of America) for the best published science fiction of the year. The artifact itself is a transparent rectangular block in which has been suspended traces of an unspecified glittery material in a vague pinwheel configuration, thus suggesting the astronomical. That the author has never won a Nebula should not be taken as an indication that this sardonic aside results from any bitterness on his part; nor should it be taken as a comment on the frauds and scribblers who have inexplicably captured this award in years past.

"You've done it!" Tragg shrieked. "You've killed us both! We'll die horrible deaths!"

"Well, it's a problem I have," Trent said. "I've got sensitivity. Busy working on that. I've done pretty well with raising my consciousness, but I've got problems with compassion. I just can't seem to work any up."

The front window had darkened. Ferocious yowling came from somewhere outside. The house began to shake.

The color drained from Tragg's face. "No!"

Ruthven sat down heavily. "Boy, have I been taken to the cleaners."

"You scammed yourself," Trent said.

Ruthven nodded ruefully.

Tragg bolted from the room.

"Don't leave the Circle!" Ruthven warned. "It'll just be worse."

But Tragg was already out the door.

The shaking increased as did the usual demonic sound effects.

"I'm not finished yet," Ruthven said.

"Oh?"

"Now that I have power freed up . . ."

A hideous scream came from downstairs.

"Good luck," Trent said on his way out the door.

He had to step over something very distasteful in the vestibule. It was quite a mess.

Outside, the street looked the same. The beech trees were budding. It was early spring, and the air was kind.

"It's a beautiful day in the neighborhood," he said as he walked back to the main street.

CHAPEL

THE MUSIC SWELLED to a crescendo, the sopranos in the chorus hitting the highest note in the symphony, the Mahler No. 2.*

The funeral had been going on for some time and people were getting fidgety. Nobody really understood why the musical program had to drag on so long. The music was fine, true; but there can be too much of the finer things of life. . . .

However, that's the way the king had wanted it. His will and testament contained detailed plans for his funeral, and they were being followed to the letter.

Everyone was in attendance: the castle nobility—lords and ladies all, arrayed in their finest mourning, mostly black with a flash of color accent here and there.

The family: Incarnadine's legal wife, Zafra, unveiled and in white, and her two children, Brandon and Belicia. (Zafra was not Queen, though Incarnadine had championed her

*Of course the second Mahler symphony bears the traditional subtitle "Music for Dead People." Sorry. This *will* be the last footnote. Promise.

cause in chancery court. The case had been pending for twelve years. Zafra was a commoner and—well, there was no end of legal bones of contention here. Still, the marriage was licit, and Brandon was heir apparent.)

And of course, the castle Guests. There were many, including a few of questionable humanity. Costumes ran the gamut from medieval to futuristic.

The castle staff: cooks, chambermaids, footmen, valets, scullery maids, the lot.

The castle tradespeople: smiths and cordwainers and seamstresses and such.

The professionals: librarians, solicitors, physicians, and scribes.

And functionaries and bureaucrats and those sorts.

The odd unclassifiable.

They were all there. The chapel was stuffed from nave to apse, with standing-room-only in the transepts.

And of course, the priests. Seventy acolytes assisted twelve High Priests as they all sang and chanted, knelt and invoked, recited and mumbled. Clouds of incense reached the roof timbers, and galaxies of candles blazed.

It was a very elaborate affair. Very nice. The corpse looked so natural. You could hardly believe he was dead. Nice job the undertaker did, wasn't it? The music was beautiful (Is this the last movement?).

Suddenly, amidst all this pageantry, the corpse sat bolt upright.

First came a shocked silence. The orchestra played on for a few more measures—the chorus cut out first, then the choirmaster craned his head around and fell off the podium.

There began some screaming. Women, mostly. Some fainted. A few men screamed and fainted. One of the High Priests fell over backwards, knocked over two smoking braziers, causing a minor fire.

The corpse—the king—rubbed his eyes. He looked down at himself and the casket he was sitting in. Then he stared around: at the priests, at the congregation, up at the choir loft, and back to the congregation.

And he said, with considerable pique, *"Ye gods! Can't a fellow take a little nap around here?"*

GAMING HALL

DALTON AND LORD PETER were at it again, at odds over a charming little endgame, one worthy of Russian chessmasters. Lord Peter had castled early; Dalton had fortified himself with a Sicilian defense. It was a defensive game; and, as a pitching duel in baseball, it was academically interesting—very admirable, but not a lot of fun.

Linda was settled in a wing chair, doing cross-stitch and absently watching flames blazing in the fireplace. Seated in the chair opposite was Melanie McDaniel, stringing her guitar.

Snowclaw sat at a card table working a crossword puzzle. He had recently learned to read English and had become literate in an astonishingly short time. Deena sat at the same table with a fresh deck, trying to remember some card tricks she once knew.

"Damn!"

Lord Peter had just lost his queen.

"Sorry, old boy," Dalton consoled.

Lord Peter sighed. "Should have seen that one coming across the drawbridge."

Otherwise, the mood was subdued.

There were more Guests in the Gaming Hall. In a far corner, a few of the younger men were engaged in a fantasy role-playing game. Something about oubliettes and mythical saurians.

"Is it winter out?" Linda suddenly asked.

Melanie was busy with tightening a string. "Huh?"

"The castle's so big sometimes you're not even aware of what season it is."

"I dunno. Why do you need to know? You can find any season you want inside the castle."

"I know, but . . . that's different. Somehow. It feels like winter. Does it feel like winter to you?"

"I went out into the desert today, and it was hot. That's all I know."

"You like deserts, don't you?"

"Yeah, I do. I lived in Phoenix when I was little. There was a lot of desert down there, then."

"I like forest aspects best. Trees, brooks, toadstools, fresh air."

"All that's nice. I don't know what it is I like about the desert. All I know is that it's quiet and still and hot. And I like it. And I like cactuses. Cacti."

"'Cactuses' is okay," Linda said. "They're sharp and prickly, though. Don't much care for them." Linda did a few stitches, then stopped. "I still think it's winter out. Maybe I'll go up into one of the turrets and look."

"They're too high for me. I get dizzy."

"You afraid of heights?"

"Sort of," Melanie said. "You going to go look and see what season it is?"

Linda thought about it. "Maybe. Tomorrow."

"I'll go with you if you want."

"Okay. I'll let you know."

Melanie plucked the new string, then started tuning it.

Holding out a fan-spread deck to Snowclaw, Deena Williams said, "Pick a card."

"Huh?"

"Pick a card, and I'll show you a trick."

"What do you mean, a trick?"

"I'll tell you what card you picked."

"I don't need anyone to tell me what card I picked if I pick a card."

"No, you don't understand. I'll tell you what card you picked without looking at the card."

"You mean you want me to tell you what card it is?"

"No! *I'll* tell *you* what card it is."

"But I already know what card it is."

"No, no! Snowy, listen. I'll tell you what card it is without you tellin' me or me lookin' at the card. Get it?"

"How can you do that?"

"Well, I'll show you."

"Yeah, but it'd have to be some kind of trick."

Deena rolled her eyes. "That's the *point*, you big goofy thing. It's a card trick."

"Yeah, it would have to be. So, what good is it?"

"Whaddya mean?"

"If it's a trick, then you really can't tell me what card I picked."

"Yes, I can!"

"But you said it's a trick. That means you sneak a look at it or figure it out some way with numbers or something or do tricky stuff with your hands, hiding it, and sort of like that. Right?"

Deena was mystified. "Well, for Pete's sake, that's what card tricks are all about."

"Like I said, what good is it? You can't *really* know what card I picked without doing any of that stuff. Can you?"

Deena slumped. She bent over and bumped her forehead

against the tabletop. "I don't *believe* I'm havin' this conversation."

"I don't see your problem. Hey, do you know an eight-letter word for a stupid person?"

"Yeah. 'Snowclaw.'"

"Hey. Lighten up."

"Confound it!"

Lord Peter had just lost his last knight.

"You must have some arcane strategy in mind," Dalton said. "I can't figure why you gave that up."

"Damn your eyes, I didn't bloody well give it up intentionally, and you bloody well know it!"

"Sorry. Temper, temper."

"Oh, bugger off."

After a strained silence, Lord Peter added, "Sorry, old chap. Lost it, there. Please forgive."

"Think nothing of it, my lord."

"I think I shall concede," Lord Peter said, assessing the board. "Yes, yes. All's lost. You've got me boxed in good and tight. The game's yours."

"Sorry, old bean."

"Tut, tut. Good game, damn good." Lord Peter let out a breath and sat back. Then he yawned. "Pardon me. Past my bedtime. Been having a devil of a time sleeping lately."

"Oh? Any reason you can think of?"

"Been having strange dreams."

"What sort?"

"Don't know. Can't remember them. Never remember dreams."

"How do you know they're strange?"

"They wake me up."

"Try a glass of warm milk."

"Hate milk."

"Well, go see Mirabilis."

"Won't take pills."

"Well, you're out of luck, my friend."

"It's nothing, really. Hardly life-threatening."

"Well, you need your rest. You should try a pill, at least."

"No, I shall down three drams of Scotch whisky before bed tonight. I should think that will fix it right up."

"There you go. The old remedies are best."

"Now, that's the first sensible thing you've said all week."

Melanie had finished tuning, and was now idly strumming a chord.

"Play something," Linda suggested.

"Oh, not really in the mood. You ever going to tell me about your love life?"

"I don't have one. Except in my dreams."

"Dreams, yeah."

Gene Ferraro came striding in.

"Evening, folks."

"Hi, Gene!" Melanie said brightly. "What've you been doing lately?"

"Not a whole hell of a lot."

Gene took a seat at the card table and commandeered the deck, which Deena had given up on.

Linda asked, "Find any interesting aspects lately?"

"Nope."

"Have any good adventures?"

Gene searched his memory. "Nnnnnope."

Melanie sighed. "This is the point where someone usually says, 'Are we having fun yet?' "

"I'm having a good time," Snowclaw said simply. "I need a word or a phrase that means 'perilous aspect.' Ten letters."

"Can't help," Linda said. "I'm terrible at crossword puzzles."

Shuffling the deck, Gene looked around at his fellow Guests.

"Well, folks. Anyone for bridge?"

King's Chambers

Incarnadine, Lord of the Western Pale and King of the Realms Perilous, woke up with a start.

"Huh?"

He sprang to a sitting position and looked wildly around the room. It took a moment to focus.

Yes. His bedchamber, in the castle. He was home. Everything was all right. He was safe.

"Gods. What a monster of a dream."

He threw off the covers and arose from the royal bed. Naked, he stalked across the room and went into the privy, closing the door.

Water pipes gurgled.

At length he emerged in a red woolen dressing gown. He went to a dressing table and poured himself a drink from an earthen pitcher. He sipped. Scowling, he poured the rest of the tepid water back into the pitcher.

He moved to the liquor cabinet and examined the offerings. Finally selecting a bottle of rye, he served himself a stiff drink and spritzed a tiny bit of soda into it.

He tossed the whole thing off in one go. Grimacing, he put the glass down.

He considered going back to bed, but reconsidered.

He turned on a lamp. The red leather chair next to the bookshelf looked comfortable. He eased into it, picked up the current book he was reading, a murder mystery, and lifted his slippered feet onto the footstool.

Settling back, he took a deep breath. He opened the book to the spot the bookmark marked and began reading.

After a moment he lowered the book and frowned pensively. He tried to remember the dream, but couldn't.

He shook his head.

"I have *got* to stop eating those damned submarine sandwiches so late at night."

FINAL EXAM

THIS TEST WILL count as 60% of your final grade. Read each question carefully. Extra points will be awarded for cogent reasoning, elegant prose style, political correctness, and neatness. When you are finished, close your test booklet and sit quietly until everyone is done. Do not gloat at sluggards. Do *not* pare your nails. You may begin.

Write a 500-word essay on any three of the following:

Question No. 1

Does that author cheat who ends a story with ". . . and it was all a dream"? Discuss what "cheat" could mean in this context. Is an author's desperate need for cash any excuse?

Question No. 2

Trace the roots of the literature of the fantastic to its ancient origins. Is it true that an appreciable percentage of the aficionados of this sort of literature, down through the ages, have had a weight problem and tended to favor the wearing of bib overalls?

Question No. 3

Give a brief summary of the history of Tierra del Fuego, outlining its political, economic, cultural, and social development, and tell why this tiny, brave nation is important to the growth of genre fantasy in the last third of the 20th century.

Question No. 4

Of what significance, if any, is the nonsense phrase "Tekeli-li," and what could the author possibly have had in mind? Explain "mind" in this context.

Question No. 5

Why must I be a teenager in love?

Question No. 6

Briefly outline the historical development of castles in western Europe. What, if anything, do they have to do with cannoli? By the way, is "cannoli" singular or plural? Are the vanilla kind better than the chocolate?

Question No. 7

Tell why you like reading stories about dragons and castles and fairies and that sort of thing. Have you ever read, say, *A la recherche du temps perdu* by Marcel Proust? Compare and contrast this book with any genre fantasy novel and explain why a writer would spend 30 pages describing how he rolls over in bed (no kidding). Why do the French think so highly of Jerry Lewis?